Top Down Day
1 family, 3 days, 4 perspectives

Nicole Overby

DESCRIPTION

A simple phone call has Dawn's world turned upside down.

The most important person in her life is now fighting for his life. As the walls start enclosing around her, she battles between protecting her children and her husband. Emotions are high and patience is running thin.

Whose opinion matters most in a situation like this?

What will tomorrow bring?

This book walks readers through some of the scariest moments in life. It brings to light different emotions and internal conflicts when death is near. The story is a great guide for those finding themselves in traumatic situations and wondering if their feelings are out of line.

TOP DOWN DAY

DEDICATION

To my hero,

May this book achieve your goal of becoming an author one day and may your memory live on forever. I strive to make you proud every day of my life.

My deepest love,

Colie Olie

"But oh who needs that sentimental bullshit, anyway" -Cold Chisel

ACKNOWLEDGMENTS

I have to start by thanking my mom and siblings. I would have never written this without your support and love. Your encouragement is what pushed me to finish writing our story. I hope my work makes you proud.

To my amazing neighbor, who has probably read this story more than anyone else. Thank you for reviewing this book with an editor's eye and providing the constructive feedback I needed to hear. More importantly, thank you for the friendship your family has provided.

A very special thank you to my loving boyfriend; I don't know how you put up with me. When I start to doubt myself, you bring me back on track. Without you, I wouldn't be where I am today.

Finally, thank you to all of those who helped my family and I get to this place of happiness and peace.

PROLOGUE

The ringing is loud; ear-piercing loud. I look around anxiously trying to pinpoint the source of the sound.

The hands aren't moving, not even the long one. *This clock has to be broken.* The talking in the room has gone silent. I can't even catch the shouting of his vitals anymore.

My sister isn't gasping for air in between each tear and I can't hear my brother trying to console her. *What is going on?*

I turn vigorously, searching for my mom, searching for the sound, searching for answers.

Brandon is all I can see-- he is so close to my face, trying to comfort me, when really I just need him to get the fuck out of my way. *Where is my mom? Where is the sound? Where is the rewind button?* Everything goes black.

Welcome to my nightmare.

Part I

FRIDAY

MARCH 22ND

TOP DOWN DAY

- ONE -

Natalie

Well, this is a shit show.

I don't understand why it is so hard for volunteers to show up on time. This is the fifth open house of the academic year, so it isn't like this is new for everyone. If you *personally* selected your volunteer time, I assume you checked your calendar to ensure you can show up for the time you *personally* selected!!

I need to keep reminding myself-- *only one more event; I can do this.*

I hear the phone in my purse ringing on the table across from me. *Shit! I forgot to turn off my phone.* I dart over to mute the sound and see it's a call from my mom. *I wish it was a call from one of the late volunteers with a believable story about how their house mysteriously caught on fire, and that is why they're reasonably 45 minutes late.*

I think this job is turning me into a bitter person.

One more event; I remind myself, as I mute the call and turn off my phone.

|SIX HOURS EARLIER|

Dawn

The clock reads 6:02 AM. *Great--I'm already two minutes behind schedule.*

13

"I have to leave," I call out searching for my keys. "I'll be home around 3 PM."

"Sounds good! See you later, Tim Allen!" Corey laughs out as he leans in for a kiss.

I roll my eyes, grab my coffee, and head towards the door. Google Maps begins to direct me to the Habitat for Humanity build. This is my third year helping Corey's company with their sponsored house. I'm grateful for his job since it's allowed me to be a stay-at-home mom for all these years, so occasionally volunteering my time is the least I can do.

As I sit in the notorious Charlotte traffic, a news update pops up on my phone screen about the North Dakota vs. Duke game. I shoot Corey a playful text, "could the North Dakota game be the one that blows everyone's bracket?"

My phone pings quickly with a response, "Tough draw for the Bison."

How did I marry a Montana native who has a love for North Dakota sports teams, of all places? My face warms as the smile creeps across my face, my head still shaking back and forth. *At least we could meet in the middle with the Denver Broncos.*

We met in Denver at work after mutual friends introduced us nearly thirty years ago. Our three beautiful children were born there, and at times, I wonder if he misses it as much as I sometimes do.

Kristen

The ringing of the alarm clock can probably wake up half of the residents in my apartment complex. *I'm sure everyone appreciates a six in the morning wake up call from the nursing students needing to head to clinical.* It doesn't help that I always have to be forty-five minutes early to everything.

As I'm rolling out of bed, Midnight greets me with a meow below. I can rationalize staying in bed five more minutes if it's dedicated to spending personal time with him. Plus, I've decided to go home for the weekend so I deserve this extra time in my own bed with my kitten. Just as I start resting my eyes, I hear a small ping from the dresser.

I bet it's Lindsey checking if I've gotten out of bed yet. We've been roommates for two years now, and we almost know each others' routine better than we know our own.

| 9:12 AM |

Thomas

The airport is full today. *Unusually full.*

"What day is it?" I ask as I search for my credit card.

"Umm, Friday," the barista answers confusingly.

"I mean what's the date today? The 19th maybe?"

"Oh! It's **March 22nd**," I respond after glancing down at my Apple watch.

It clicks in my head as I pay for my Starbucks caramel macchiato-- some colleges are still on spring break. March is a busy time for family travel. It adds great entertainment for the weekly business travelers.

While drinking my coffee, I look around at all of the families in the terminal. *I really should write down half of the entertainment I witness every week; I would have a full years' worth of stand-up.* The family boarding at the gate next to me catches my attention. I can hear the attendant trying to explain that their group number hasn't been called yet. I can't help but shake my head as I continue to sip my drink.

My comic piece would go something like… "Airports should designate a timeout area for those who try to board with a different group. An area for those who think the rules don't apply to them, with red flashing lights to intensify the public shame."

15

I catch myself laughing at my own joke.

Dawn

My Apple watch starts buzzing while I'm on top of the roof putting on the shingles. I glance down and notice the call's from Corey. *That's odd.* He knew I was going to Habitat for the day and would be tied up with the home build.

"I have to take this." I explain to George, the contractor, as I climb down the ladder, hoping to find a quiet place. The nailing is too loud; I won't be able to hear a thing he says.

"Hey, everything okay?" I answer trying to balance the phone on my shoulder.

Corey's breathing is slow and heavy.

"I think... I need you to come home."

The hesitation in his voice is obvious.

"What's wrong, Corey?" My heart begins to race.

"I threw up a little bit of blood."

My vision begins to fade as I listen to him over the phone.

"Nothing to stress about..."

Even with the alarming news, his voice remains calm.

"but I think you should come take me to the emergency room just in case."

His last few words keep ringing in my ears... *"just in case."*

Squeezing my eyes shut, I try to regain focus. Searching for my car, I respond, "I'm leaving now. I will see you in 40 minutes. Don't move."

I can feel my mind starting to run a million miles per hour. *Blood! He threw up blood!* Once in my car, I realize I never told George I'm leaving. I roll down the window and yell, "Family emergency! Have to go!" I watch the confusion grow across his face, but I decide I'll explain it to him later, once Corey is home and feeling better.

I look down at the speedometer, reaching 80 miles per hour. *What am I doing? I need to calm down!* I begin to ease my lead-foot just as I see the car stereo light up with a phone call coming through. It's Corey again.

"Dawn, I don't think I'm going to make it until you get back. I need you to call an ambulance."

I can hear his voice getting weaker, my heart beating harder.

What do I do?! I'm not going to make it. My call will pick up EMTs in the Charlotte area. Think, Dawn. I can't see the road anymore, all I can envision is Corey at the house, so helpless.

"Okay, okay. I, um, I need to call the neighbor. So, so dispatch sends EMTs near you, not me. Okay, Corey, I'm going to call Marianne."

I'm sure he can hear the worry growing in each word.

Before I even let him answer, I hang up and call Marianne. The rings go on for an eternity before I get her voicemail. "Fuck!" I scream out as I slam on the brakes just in time to avoid smashing into the car in front of me. I don't know if I'm more pissed at this unnecessary traffic light in the middle of the busiest road, or knowing I'm wasting precious time trying to get ahold of a fucking neighbor. *Jean has to be home.* I dial her number as fast as my shaky fingers will allow me. The car horn behind me rings in my ears. "Fuck off!" I yell with an accompanying middle finger. *Holy shit, what am I doing?*

I try taking a few deep breaths to calm me down as I listen to the long, unanswered rings.

"Hey Dawn, how are you!" Jean cheerfully calls out.

Jean is also a stay-at-home mom. She's the mom with the Cricut and carpooling kids to hockey games. *I remember when that was me.* We'd been meaning to catch up recently, but our schedules are polar opposites now that my kids are all on their own. *I knew she'd answer.* She probably thought it

17

was time to finally catch up.

"Jean, listen. I need you to call an ambulance for Corey." My tone probably startles her.

"What! Is everything okay?!"

I want to yell back, "Yes, Jean, everything's fine. Corey's just testing the response time for dispatchers to make sure we live in a safe neighborhood."

Sarcasm will waste time. Anger will waste time. I know this.

"Jean, listen. Call the ambulance." I hang up before I can hear another comment that will send me completely over the edge.

I dial Corey back. "I called Jean. She's calling an ambulance. Stay on the phone with me. How are you doing?" I sound like a general shouting out orders.

Don't sound panicked; you have to stay calm for him. Everything is going to be fine; it always is. Breathe, Dawn, breathe. I almost miss Corey's response because my inner pep talk is so loud.

"I'll be okay. How's the house, handyman?"

I swear I can see the smile creeping over his face as he laughs at his own question. *Why is he always so calm? Why can't I be more like him? I always overreact and let my mind race to the worst imaginable situation.*

A deep cough follows his laugh, but it's distant. *He's covering the speaker with his hand. He's trying to mask the noise.* He doesn't want me to hear, so I shake my head trying to erase the sound and keep the conversation going. Keep him focused.

"Not bad. Just working on my skills so I can make improvements to our home."

"Of course you are." A shorter, hesitant chuckle follows his words. *He's being careful.*

I hear the ambulance sirens and I know the EMTs have finally arrived. I listen while the EMTs ask Corey question after question, trying to assess the situation. Corey explains how he's such a needy husband, making me leave my event early. I don't fight the smile appearing on my face as I listen to the laughter of strangers. He always makes me sound so important, when in actuality, without him our family would have nothing. *Nothing.* I hear the EMTs telling Corey he's being taken to our local hospital for further assessment of the bleeding.

I hear the strangers going over each move before it happens.

"Okay, Corey."

Noises ruffling, but I can't make out what it is.

"We're going to get you sitting upright."

He must be in bed.

"Bring you onto a stretcher."

Or is he laying on the bathroom floor?

"Bring you out of the garage, into the ambulance."

No he had to be in bed. He isn't that bad.

"Are you ready?"

The directions help calm me down as I can envision the play-by-play. But then, suddenly, I don't feel so calm anymore. No one's talking; no one's laughing anymore. I can barely hear anyone. *What happened?* I check the volume on my phone and cling onto the steering wheel. My knuckles slowly turning white.

"Corey, Corey, Corey!" I hear the stranger's voice suddenly call out.

"What is happening?!" I yell into the phone, praying Corey put me on speaker phone.

"Corey, come back to us."

More noise.

"Come on, Corey!"

What the fuck is going on! The lead-foot returns as I rush to meet the ambulance at the hospital.

A new voice calls out, "Bill, lift his head up!"

The panic in their voices is piercing.

"He isn't responsive-- his blood pressure is dropping!"

Now I know there are three strangers in my house with my husband. Three strangers I'm depending on.

"Keep trying!"

The orders continue.

"Try this!"

"Try that!"

Yet, none of them are telling me what exactly is going on. I try to focus on the road, knowing there is nothing I can do until I get to the hospital. *I'm useless until I'm there, right next to him, helping him.*

"There you go! He's coming back."

Thank God.

I listen to the muffling on the other line, trying to make out a single word.

"Welcome back Corey. We lost you there for a minute."

I hear one of them take a slow, deep breath. *Are they as relieved as I am?*

"We're almost ready to get you to the ambulance; we need you to stay with us. Try focusing on your breathing."

I vaguely hear the strangers reading off his vitals and approximately how much blood he's lost. My ears are ringing, and I keep pressing my finger into them to stop the buzzing. *I need to be listening, paying attention to every detail.*

Then, I hear his voice and the noise disappears.

"Don't worry honey, I'm not dead yet." Corey laughs those words so clearly. My shoulders fall, and I feel like I can finally breathe again. *He knew I was still listening through the phone.* Of course he did, I think as I fall into a reverie. *Why does he always seem to make jokes during the worst possible times?*

I daze off to a memory a few months ago when he had to have foot surgery. He's battled with his feet for several years, but the doctors were hopeful this was going to be the final surgery. The surgery was to realign his ankle to avoid pressure points in his feet. When he filled out his pre-surgery paperwork he put down "Aquaman" as the name he would prefer to be called. I'll never forget the look on the nurse's face when he came to get him for surgery. "Are you ready to be taken back for surgery, *Aquaman?"*

I can't help but grin as I think of the memory. *We will get through this, it will be okay; it's always been okay.*

| 9:38 AM |

<u>Kristen</u>

"Hi. You have reached the cellphone of Dawn Owen. I can't come to…"

I hang up the phone. I was calling my mom as soon as I reached the hospital's parking lot. Clinicals were cancelled today. Dr. Murphy must have known the class was itching to start our weekend. As I reach my car, I decide to give Natalie a call-- the only phone number I've ever memorized.

Must be a twin thing.

"The number you have called has a full voicemail box and cannot accept any messages at this time."

I swear she leaves herself voicemails so no one else can. As much as I love her, she definitely pisses me off. *Why isn't anyone answering my calls?* I decide to give Lindsey a ring.

"Hey, girl!"

Finally, someone answers!

"Hey, have you left for the weekend yet?"

"Nope. Have you?"

"Nope! Clinicals were cancelled, and I could use a distractor from the amount of work my professors have assigned."

I slide into the driver-side seat and place the keys into the ignition.

"Haha! I can relate. I'm convinced our professors don't want us to enjoy our weekends for the rest of the semester. Want to grab coffee at Java?"

"Yes, please! See you in 20?"

"Perfect!"

She's always such a good roommate.

| 10:00 AM |

Dawn

Why does Candy Crush have the loudest music? I guarantee if the app developers did market research they would come to the conclusion that 80- 90% of users play the game in areas where music isn't appreciated or appropriate.

I quickly silence the music as I apologize with my eyes to Corey. He doesn't seem bothered by the sound, but I can tell he's uncomfortable in the emergency room bed. I was hoping this game would distract me from thinking about how long we've been waiting. *How did it get this bad? Did he seem sick this morning before I left?*

I stand up and walk over to his bedside.

"Anything I can do?" I ask, but knowing there is nothing.

"No, I..."

Before he can even finish his sentence I watch his face turn pale. *Something is wrong, very wrong.* In slow motion, I watch the blood spill out of his mouth before it hits me. I look down at my shirt. Clumps of dark blood are splattered across my chest. Before I can manage a word, Corey murmurs, "I'm so sorry" while blood is still dripping from the corners of his mouth.

I want to cry as I watch the embarrassment rise across his face. *He's sorry? He's sorry!? Is he kidding me! I'm sorry! I'm sorry he is in this much pain. I'm sorry I left this morning. I'm sorry these nurses don't seem to think this is an emergency!*

"HEEELP!" I cry out.

Nurses come circling in to clean up the mess along with a doctor. The nurses assure me he is next in line for the CT scan. The doctor explains that the CT scan will give them a clearer picture of where the blood is coming from in his body. He rambles on about how once they figure this out, it will be a relatively easy procedure to stop the bleeding. I remember my coworker once told me her mother had been admitted to the hospital for blood in her stool. Once they found the source of the bleeding, it was only a matter of an hour before it stopped. Her mother fully recovered and returned back to her normal life in less than a week. This thought gives me hope, and I cling onto it.

Once the mess is cleaned up, everyone leaves and we're back to where we started. Waiting for this miraculous scan to tell us what needs to be done to get him feeling better.

I grab my phone and send a quick text to Kristen. "hi sweetie. sorry i missed your call. call on your way home xoxo." I can't tell her. *Not yet.*

I decide to go check with the nurses to see exactly how much longer until the CT scan. The walls all look the same in the emergency room. *It never makes sense to me why hospitals have to look so white, so cold.* As I'm turning the corner, I hear a nurse dressed in darker scrubs yell out, "Code Blue!" A breeze of air brushes pass me as the nurses change direction and sprint past me. I make a mental note to say a prayer for the code blue patient after I get an update on the wait time. "Room 2B" the lead nurse yells again. *Room 2B. I couldn't have heard that right.*

Everything goes fuzzy and the ringing in my ears is slowly coming back. *Where is this noise coming from? Did they really say Room 2B?*

My feet are picking up speed but I can't physically feel myself move. As nurses huddle around the room, I find myself being pushed to the outside, only able to peer through the window.

One nurse calls out, "He's seizing!"

"Get the restraints," answers a different nurse.

Why are they restraining him? I look frantically at the screaming monitor; his blood pressure is dropping drastically. *He must have thrown up again.*

"Corey, relax. We are trying to help you, Corey."

This nurse sounds so calm, so collected. She must have several years of experience, but she doesn't look very old.

"These are our friendship bracelets, Corey."

She keeps repeating his name like she's known him for years. It makes each order more personal, more meaningful.

"We put them on special patients, Corey."

Corey won't buy any of this crap. Why is she talking to him like a three-year-old? I need to get in there! I need to stop this!

"Stop!" I cry out as I push myself into the room.

"Who is this?" the doctor yells out.

"I'm his freaking wife!"

"Listen ma'am, you either need to calm down, or get out of here."

Don't tell me to leave. I'm his wife, damn it! I settle for a head nod since he seems adamant about me leaving if I don't calm down.

The young nurse turns towards me, with pleading eyes, asking, "Do you think you can try calming him down?"

I don't think anything is going to calm him down right now.

"We need to restrain him so we can intubate him. The bleeding is interfering with his airway."

His airway? You can do this, Dawn. You need to do this.

I shuffle between the crowd of nurses and toss my purse on the ground. I approach his bedside and reach for his shaky hands. *I hope he can't feel the shakiness in my hands or hear the fear in my voice.*

"Corey, can you hear me?"

What am I expecting? Him to answer? My heart is racing and my lungs can't get enough air.

"Relax, Corey, please. I'm right here."

Tears start to fill my eyes. *I'm not strong enough for this.*

"I'm right by your side, Corey, right here."

I'm not going anywhere.

"The doctors are trying to help you feel better. We need your muscles to stop tensing up. We need you to relax."

We need to stick this damn tube down your throat. I glance over and I see

25

the vitals slowly improve.

"There you go, Corey. Great job." I want to vomit as I say the last words. *Great job; who am I kidding? This is terrible; I'm terrible. What did I miss this morning?*

"Mrs. Owen, we're going to lightly sedate Corey to get him calmed down enough to safely slide the tube down his throat."

Sedate him?

"Once we get him intubated, we will run the CT scan."

It's about damn time this scan is happening!

I nod my head, not knowing if I'm trying to signal my acceptance or my understanding. *Do I even have a choice in all of this?* In another uncomfortable chair, I take my place as I watch the nurses administer the sedation through his IV. Everyone is shuffling around the room, well-aware of their task; some in charge of sedation while others, the tube. An older nurse, I'd guess around late thirties, slowly tips Corey's head back and that's when I see it. It's so small, so quiet. I imagine everyone else in the room misses it, too busy with their next step, but I don't. I watch the smallest tear helplessly fall out of the corner of Corey's eye and the sight of it is enough for me to lose my breath. My spine loses all strength and my chest falls to my knees. *Does he know he's in trouble?* Using my lap, I push myself up and turn my head to the window. Each hand sealing my mouth shut, keeping the sobs tightly held in. The sun is shining, the trees bright green. *I watched until I couldn't watch anymore, Corey.* I know I have to remain silent, remain calm or the doctor will kick me out of the room.

A nurse in the corner interrupts my pain, possibly because she can tell I'm seconds from completely losing it. "We need you to go back to the waiting room while we bring him back for the scan."

Is this nurse out of her mind?! I'm being quiet, I'm staying calm-- why do I have to leave? I'm not going anywhere, not now. As I look over to face her, I can tell by her cold stare she isn't changing her mind. Now my blood pressure is rising. I begin to play out the scenario if I put up a fight. *I can't waste any time, any of Corey's time. We need to know where the bleeding is coming from.*

I snatch my purse and abruptly leave the room, but not without clearly stating, "You better be fast and I want an update immediately."

I grab my phone. *I need to vent to someone, anyone. Natalie.* As the rings go unanswered, I realize I haven't told the kids we're at the hospital. It all happened so fast, and Corey never wants to worry the kids. I know he did it out of protection, but now I feel stuck between my husband and my kids.

When the call finally goes to voicemail, my phone dings with a text in our family group message. *Do I tell the kids, or do I keep the privacy wishes of my husband?*

Damn it, Corey. I wish I could talk to you. I can't do this alone.

| 12:08 PM |

Thomas

"We will begin our boarding process momentarily."

I reach for my phone and send out a quick text to the family group message. "Boarding. I will try to make dinner tonight. Love you." I double-check I have the next 3 episodes of Dexter downloaded before turning my phone to airplane mode.

"At this time, we would like to welcome all MileagePlus Premier members."

| 1:07 PM |

Natalie

As I put away the last folded tablecloth, I feel a sense of relief creep over me. I suddenly feel as if I can breathe in a full gasp of air again. I have

27

officially finished the last event for my graduate assistantship.

It's not as if I don't appreciate the position, because I definitely do. I mean it's helping me pay for my M.B.A after all, but I'm not sure I was cut out to be an event coordinator. Or at least not a university event coordinator. Maybe if I was a glamorous event coordinator where I nonchalantly meet celebrities I could handle the stress of the job, but simply organizing open houses for unamused teenagers is not for me.

I deserve a gin and tonic. Or seven.

As I start to self-indulge in my imagined celebration, I realize I need to call Brandon. He had baseball practice this afternoon, but we had plans to meet up before I head to a conference in Pittsburgh for the weekend. Three missed calls and two awaiting text messages follow the Apple logo on the screen. *I forgot my mom called right before the event this morning.* She didn't leave a voicemail, which she usually does if it's urgent. I crack a smile as I begin to wonder if she was calling about last night's recap of American Idol or about someone she ran into at the grocery store. *I'll call her back after I call Brandon.*

"Hey, babe! How was your event?"

"Eh, it was fine. Some hiccups, but whatcha gonna do! I was wondering if we were still on for Voodoo?"

"For sure. I have to put away some equipment, but I should be leaving in about 15."

"Great! See you then. Love you."

"Love you always."

He always ends the call that way, even after five years. Yet, I still feel the heat rush through my body every time I hear him proudly say, 'always.'

I throw my phone in my purse and rush to my car. *I'll call my mom in the car so it can connect to Bluetooth.*

Dawn

Sitting in the extremely stiff chair in the waiting room, my tailbone begins to send excruciating pain signals to my brain. I glance over at the surrounding families in the room. *Are they as uncomfortable as I am, or are they ignoring how unbelievably hard these chairs are?* I begin to imagine stories for all of the other red-eyed people around me. It helps distract me from reality. How ridiculous that if the patient, *your own husband,* is in the ICU you can't go in unless granted access. They changed his room after the severity of the coding and are now preparing him for the scan.

I walk to the call system and ring the nurses again.

"Hi, yes this is Dawn again. Can I come in yet?"

The nurse's initial sigh doesn't go unheard before she continues to say, "As stated fifteen minutes ago, we will personally come notify you when you are granted permission to enter the room."

"This is bullshit." I grumble under my breath as I walk back to the stiff chair.

We have been at the hospital for almost four and a half hours now. Even though it's only the afternoon, my body is convinced it's eleven o'clock at night. *This backbreaking chair won't allow me to doze off anyway so I have nothing to worry about.* Just as I begin adjusting my position for the nine hundredth time, my phone vibrates.

Natalie's goofy face appears on the screen. A smile folds onto my face when I see her. *She hasn't been home in so long, and man did I miss her.* We were so proud of her when she decided to continue her education. In all of the excitement, we forgot to realize how little time she would have to come home during her studies in Erie.

My throat tightens as the realization hits my brain. "Shit-- the kids!" I don't know if I said it out loud but several heads turn to face me. I whisper, "I'm sorry" to the other families in the waiting room as I walk down the hall near the elevators.

29

"Natalie."

I can't tell if my voice gives me away. *Damn it, Dawn; keep it together.*

"Hey Mom, sorry I missed your call. I had an open house today. I'm so exhausted, but I'm going to meet Brandon for a celebratory drink before I head to the city. I told you I have the Women in Business conference this weekend, right? So I'll head there after I see Brandon."

I must not have sounded as tired or nervous or scared or every other emotion I'm feeling as I listen to her go on and on.

"Mom? You there?"

"Yes, sorry sweetie."

I know I should tell her how excited we are that she is one step closer to finally moving down to North Carolina. We should be laughing about how some mother at the open house asked how late the library stays open while her child cringed with embarrassment. I should be telling her to go and enjoy herself with Brandon and celebrate the end of event coordinating. My brain keeps going crazy with what I should say next, but my mouth won't utter a word.

"Are you okay, Mom? Why are you being so quiet?" Natalie says with a light, accompanying laugh.

"Yes, of course!" I reply with a little too much reassurance.

"Are you sure?" Her voice sounds a little less sure.

I hear the Bluetooth disconnect. Her voice is closer and louder on the phone. I know this means she's arrived at her destination. She's minutes away from celebrating with Brandon.

This is my last chance to tell her.

I can hear Corey telling me, as he has said so many times before, "It's nothing serious, Dawn. We shouldn't involve the kids yet; they have enough on their plates."

"Natalie…" I ask, making sure she was still there after the silence from my long internal debate.

"Yeah, what's up?" she asks as I listen to the wind hitting the phone speaker, making her words muffled now.

"Dad's been admitted to the hospital; nothing too serious."

Am I trying to convince her or myself?

"He called me explaining he threw up some blood this morning; nothing too serious."

Stop saying nothing too serious!

"We wanted to get it checked out just to stay on top of things; nothing too serious."

Damn it! My eyes rolling at myself.

"But I just wanted you to know in case you couldn't reach me. Please don't tell Kristen or Thomas until we know more."

Why am I rambling on right now, not letting her get a word in? My brain's throwing out any words it can think of.

I'm waiting for Natalie to digest the information. She's always been my confidant so I know she wouldn't be tempted to tell others before I did.

"Is it serious? Don't bullshit me," she said coldly. So cold, it almost feels like a jab, as if she's insulted I didn't call her earlier. *She surely hadn't forgotten I had tried calling her hours ago and* **she didn't answer.**

"I'm, I'm really not sure," is all I can manage to say as I remember watching his body seize and his eyes roll back. I close my eyes tightly, trying to erase the image.

"Should I book a flight home?"

"No, no, no."

My head shaking at the thought.

"The doctors said once we find the source it will be fixable. I'll keep you updated."

"How much blood?"

Each question makes my heart beat faster. *Do I even know for sure?*

"Oh, nothing serious."

The words vomit out.

"Mom, stop. Please. How much blood?"

I see the nurse in the dark scrubs come out of the door from the corner of my eye. I know she's looking for me.

"Natalie, I will keep you updated. I have to go. I think they're coming to update me on the CT scan."

I make sure to emphasize before I hang up, "Don't tell your siblings, Natalie. It's nothing serious."

I really have to work on that.

- TWO -

|3:00 PM|

Thomas

I've always loved the initial feeling of the wheels touching the ground again. How remarkable flying truly is-- it brings together hundreds of people all going to the same place, yet for different purposes.

I turn my phone back to cellular and notice no responses to my text. *Come on, not one? Not even a "liked" message?* I still send a follow-up text notifying them of my arrival, even though it's obvious no one seems interested in my travel updates.

"Did you know people rush to the front of the aircraft because there's a prize for the first person to get to baggage claim to wait for their luggage?" I continue my comedy set in my head as I watch impatient flyers overcrowd the front of the plane. "Deboarding a plane is tricky when every flyer is the most important passenger and deserves to get off first." I test out the two lines in my head.

My stomach begins to rumble. *I wonder what Mom's cooking for dinner; I imagine something good since Kristen's coming home for the weekend.*

Natalie

How is this happening to me? To my mom? To my family? And half of them don't even know it's going on.

I watch others enter Voodoo as I wait by the door. I know Brandon's waiting inside for me, probably with a beer already half gone. *Why didn't I want to go inside?* He'll make me feel better; help me think it through. Stop my brain from wandering down a dark path.

33

The smell of food trucks and grease hit me as I enter the restaurant. Now I remember why I love this place so much-- cheap drinks and shitty food. Not shitty tasting food, but the shitty food where you savor every piece of a fully loaded gyro, but fifteen minutes after devouring it every ounce of your body hates you. I scanned the room for Brandon. *There he is.* His eyes meet mine and his smile warms my cheeks.

As I approach the table, I notice his half drank beer. I laugh to myself. *At least he didn't order food without me.*

"Hello beautiful," I hear him say.

"Why, hello there." I whisper as I lean in for a kiss.

"Sorry I didn't wait. The beer looked too refreshing to hold off."

I give him a smile as I watch him sip his beer. He reminds me of those quirky actors on beer commercials explaining how refreshing the brew is. Brandon is so dorky, but I love him, with everything I have.

I almost forgot about my mom's phone call as I look at him, but soon reality sets back in. *How could I have forgotten? How awful of a daughter does that make me?*

"So my mom called…" I start off as I slip into my seat.

"Turns out my dad's in the hospital."

Why did I sound so casual?

"Oh no! Really? How come? Is he okay? Are you okay?"

I could see the genuine concern on his face. He loves my family nearly as much as I do. Even with their differences, and they certainly have those-- especially when it comes to NFL football teams-- he knows how much my family means to me; therefore, they mean a lot to him, too.

"I'm not exactly sure. Mom kind of rushed off the phone. She mentioned he was throwing up some blood, but said it wasn't serious."

If one thing stuck from our conversation, it was her repeating, "It's nothing serious." I

34

knew she was lying or, at best, hiding something, but now here I am stealing her line.

"Do the doctors know where the bleeding is coming from?"

I didn't even want to think about the answer to this question. I don't know anything about arteries, organs, or what even causes a person to throw up blood. *That's Kristen's forte.* I just know throwing up blood isn't normal, and I'm okay with only knowing that much. I didn't need to know where it was coming from or what got so fucked up to even cause blood to be there in the first place.

"They were taking him to do a CT scan when she hung up. I don't think I've received an update from her about the results." *How long do these tests usually take anyways?*

I reach into my purse searching for my phone as I finish the sentence. The screen is blank-- no missed calls or texts. I open my recent calls, trying to decide if I should call my mom back for an update. *Shit. I forgot to call Kristen back.* I pause, trying to decide if I should call her back. *I better hold off; she can always tell when I'm keeping something from her.* Before I realize what I'm doing, I draft a text for my dad. *Maybe it will cheer him up.* I hit send and let my words, 'Thinking of you' travel to his phone.

"Do you have to go home this weekend?" Brandon asks, obviously still very concerned.

"Mom said it isn't there yet."

I don't even look up as I answer him. I'm now in the middle of drafting a text for my mom, "Any update on the CT scan??"

"I'm sure he'll be okay."

I've always loved Brandon's positive outlook on situations, but I'm too focused on my phone to appreciate his response.

Breaking the silence, Brandon asks, "When do you have to go into the city again?"

"Um, I'm going to drive to the hotel after I leave here."

35

Still distracted, my sentences are broken up with sighs of silence.

"The conference is all day Saturday and part of the day Sunday."

I finally look up at him and finish my thoughts.

"What are your plans for the weekend?"

Truthfully, I don't hear a word he's saying back to me. I'm too distracted by my own thoughts.

Is my mom going to keep me updated? Should I excuse myself and give her a call? Why did Kristen call me? Did Mom tell her about Dad? Should I excuse myself and give her a call?

I don't know what to do or what to think.

The ping paralyzes me in my chair. *Why weren't my fingers moving to grab my phone?* Brandon looks down at my phone placed on the table between us. We both look at the lit up screen and simultaneously read the sender of the text message-- *Mom <3 <3 <3.* His eyes rise to meet mine.

"I think you should read that," he whispers.

I read the message out loud, "CT scan complete. stomach is the source. now we know where to start, all ok here."

I feel pressure releasing from my chest as quickly as the air whistling out of a flat tire. I keep re-reading "all ok here." *I knew I was letting my mind wander too far. Brandon's right-- Dad's going to be okay. We're all going to be okay.*

<u>Kristen</u>

"Thanks for hanging out. I needed to kick-start my weekend with some girl talk!"

We ended up getting carried away with brunch, but the Java date was one-hundred percent necessary. I haven't seen much of Lindsey this semester since nursing school has slowly taken over any free time I thought I would have. *It's nice to finally catch up.*

"And I needed that double shot of espresso," shouts Lindsey as we both laugh.

"I am not looking forward to this drive home."

I lean back into the chair, letting my head fall back as I think about the upcoming boring drive.

"You driving home too?"

"Yeah, I'm going to head back to our place to grab my bags then I'll start the drive."

"I should stop complaining about my drive, then! My hour-long trip is starting to seem a lot better when I think about your four-hour drive," I tease, as I really did pity her long drive. She'd been slowly moving her things back home as the semester got closer to an end.

"Haha! It's not too bad. I have some podcasts downloaded to help drown out the misery... but... I better head out, my family is expecting me to make it for dinner."

I give her a hug goodbye and call out, "Safe travels. Let me know when you finally make it home!" before getting in my car.

With Google Maps all loaded up for directions home, I send a text to the family group message, "On my way home- can't wait to see everyone!" Guilt creeps up after I send the text. I keep forgetting Natalie won't be joining us this weekend. *I shouldn't have said "everyone."* My guilt reminds me that I never heard from her or my mom. I'm surprised my mom hasn't called minimally three times asking for any specialty items at the grocery store or my ETA. I send her an individual text, "Excited to see you! Love you." I'm sure I'll get something back in response. An instant response comes across my screen. Thomas sends back a gif of a baby all excited. *I can't wait to see him; he's been so busy with his new consulting job, I can't remember the last time we've really talked.*

I look down at my phone. I would arrive around 4 PM. The Charlotte Outlets were only a few miles out of the way. I decide to add one short stop on the route back home to break up the drive.

Dawn

"Dawn Owen?" the nurse asks.

"How is he doing?" I blurt out as I stand up from my chair.

"We did the CT scan and can tell the source of the bleeding is coming from his stomach. However, there is too much blood to see the direct cause. We're going to do another procedure to find the exact source. The doctor will be out shortly to explain the next steps."

"The stomach," I repeat back to her.

"The stomach is the source. That's good we know the source." I keep repeating back to her, or to me, I'm not exactly sure who I'm telling anymore. *This is a step in the right direction. We know the source.*

It's almost as if the nurse in the dark scrubs can see my brain working through the news. She watches as I take the only source of information I've been given and hold onto it with everything I have, with all of my hope.

"Also…" she mumbles, "does your husband have a living will?"

My eyebrows narrow as her words approach me, digesting her question. *What the hell! Why does she need to know this? Why would she ask me this right now?*

"Um, yes?"

My vision goes to the lockbox in our closet. I can see the box opening, the shoved papers all crumbled inside.

"Unfortunately, we will need you to go get the living will and bring it back to the hospital."

Her eyes traveling up and down my face.

"I'm sorry, it's a standard procedure."

Her eyes break mine as she finishes her sentence.

Leave the hospital, drive home, and come back? No way. No freaking way!

I look her directly in her eyes, as firm as I can, and respond, "I live 27 minutes away from the hospital."

I wonder if my face is turning red.

"It will be over an hour until I return."

I've done everything they've asked so far, but this, I'm not doing this. I don't care what they say.

"I understand, Mrs. Owen. I wish it were up to me. Could you possibly call someone to pick it up and bring it here?"

Who am I supposed to ask to go into my house, open my safe, and grab his will? How do I even begin to explain why I need it?

"I can certainly try, but I'm not sure I can get it."

The nurse starts to turn, accepting my response for now, and walks away. She seems detached from what she's telling me. It's as if she doesn't care that every word she speaks breaks me a little more inside. Her face did seem tired, and her pace is slow. *Maybe it's been a long day already?* I try to remember if she mentioned if she'd been here for a while. *Is she new to these hours? Is she fresh out of school?* Right as I'm trying to guess her age, she turns around. *Was I saying this all out loud?*

"Oh, and Mrs. Owen."

What now?

"Do you have anyone to join you in the waiting room?"

She pauses, allowing me time to think.

"Maybe a family member or friend?"

"I'm okay. Corey wouldn't want anyone else waiting on him."

39

She sighs. "I think you need to call someone. I can explain what's going on so you don't have to, but I really think you need to call someone. This might be a long road ahead of you and it'll be helpful to have someone to lean on."

Lean on. It stings. I know she didn't mean for it to, but it does.

"Thank you, but I'm okay."

Her eyes don't look as tired anymore. I feel her pity radiate towards me. *Why can't I get a read on this woman?*

"Call someone," she firmly states, almost as if she's scolding me.

Laughter starts to grow in my throat as I try to hold it down. *Call someone. Who does she think I can call? The same person who is supposed to be getting Corey's will? This woman doesn't know me, doesn't know my family,* **doesn't know Corey.**

| 5:00 PM |

Natalie

I take the last sip of my unsweetened ice tea, listening to the straw slurp at the empty cup. *I wasn't in the mood for a drink anymore.* I'm dreading the drive into the city. The weather always makes traveling in Erie so difficult, no matter what time of the year it is. I look up at Brandon.

"I better head out" I let out.

"Yeah, yeah, yeah. I know. Let me walk you out."

The air seems colder as we exit the restaurant. March brings along strange weather in Erie.

"Call me when you arrive at your hotel."

"I plan on getting some homework done tonight, but I'll send you a text once I get settled."

"Okay, okay. Drive safely."

"Love you."

I know what comes next.

"Love you always."

He gives me a wink and closes my car door for me. I watch him walk towards his car. Before opening his door, he turns around back to me and signals for me to roll the window down.

"Keep me updated on your dad. He's going to be okay, Natalie."

"I know."

Rolling up the window, I let the last rush of cold air into my car before heading off.

Do I though?

Dawn

The elevator dings. I watch my dad slowly appear behind the opening doors. His eyes are so wide behind his glasses, as if he's seen a ghost. I did finally agree to call someone to come wait with me, with the contingency that the lead nurse did all of the talking. I feel guilty that I didn't explain it to him earlier. He's had a rough year, full of countless visits to the hospitals and even funeral homes. My dad's the youngest of eight children, and it seems 2019 is the year everyone's either having a heart attack or being diagnosed with cancer. *It's been a shit year. That is for sure.*

"Dawn." I can hear the concern in his voice as he gets closer.

Why does everyone feel the need to tiptoe around me?

"Hey, Dad."

His hug instantly makes me want to cry. Let it all out; give myself a

41

second to panic. But I don't. I take a breath and pull it all back in.

"Thanks for coming. I hate bothering you, but the nurse told me to call someone, and I didn't know who else to call."

"No bother at all."

His grip on my shoulders is tight.

"The nurse on the phone seems nice."

I'm not sure if I would go as far as calling her nice.

He picks the seat right next to me and continues to say, "Any updates? How are you doing?"

How do I begin to answer that question? I haven't even taken a moment to really think about how I'm feeling. I've been so focused on Corey; he's more important right now.

"You know, hanging in there." I avoid eye contact as I answer, hoping he can't detect the lies rolling off of my tongue.

He places his hand back on my shoulder. It brings me back to being a teenager, needing my dad's protection. We don't say another word, but at least we wait together for an update. *I hate to admit it, but I'm glad the nurse pushed me to call someone.* Even though we aren't speaking, it brings comfort to know I'm not alone awaiting the unknown in this uncomfortable waiting room. The companionable silence is the slightest bit more bearable.

I listen to the elevator ding once more. Out of the corner of my eye, I see Marianne. She's always so put together. She lightens the room with her smile.

"How's Santa Claus doing?" she asks as she hands me the manila folder. I let out a laugh, and it feels so damn good.

Marianne and her husband often joke that Corey is Santa Claus. They never see him, but know he has to exist, despite physical proof. Corey's been unusually busy with work lately. The company he's worked for his entire career decided to spin off a new business, and Corey was asked to help get it established. It's quite an honor, and even when he tries to make it sound like it isn't a big deal to join the team, I know Corey's so proud of himself. *We all are so proud of him.*

I know the living will is in the folder she handed me without opening it. *Such a thoughtful touch to disguise it.* She always thinks one step ahead of everyone else.

"He's doing better! Thanks for bringing this; the nurses said it was just for precautionary measures. Always needing to protect their asses!"

What the hell am I saying? Is Corey doing better? Did the nurses ever say it was precautionary measures? Now I can't keep the story straight in my head. I can't tell if I'm lying or telling the truth. I look down at my shaking hands. I squeeze my fingers together to remind myself I'm not dreaming. *I need to get my story together.*

"Let me go get you and your dad some food."

"No, Marianne. That is so not necessary! We won't be here much longer."

Did the nurses tell me that?

"Oh stop, I'll be back shortly!"

She went back to the elevator doors. I turn to my dad, who's looking at me confused. The story he was given thirty minutes ago sounded completely different than what I just told Marianne. The nurse told my dad about the seriousness of the amount of blood Corey had lost. She told him to come right away so I didn't have to process the information alone, *make decisions alone.* I have no idea why I'm trying to be nonchalant with Marianne. *I know she would understand; I know she would be there for me.* But I don't want to bother her any more than I already have.

Before I can form a sentence to explain myself, the nurse comes out from the ICU doors, but this time a doctor accompanies her.

"Mrs. Owen, this is Dr. Kellie, the ICU doctor."

I can tell the nurse is pleased to see my dad has joined me in the waiting room as they approach us.

43

"Hello, Mrs. Owen."

He extends his hand for me to shake. *Just get to the point.*

"Unfortunately, your husband is still actively bleeding."

He gives a moment to let the news set in. A moment for me to lose my breath. A moment for my head to start spinning.

"Really, the best option is for us to do interventional radiology, which we call IR."

He no longer spares any time before diving into the details of the procedure.

"We'll use image guidance to go in through his groin and find the exact source of his bleeding in his stomach. IR is a minimally invasive treatment and it's our best option. Of course, we can take you back before the procedure so you can see Corey if you would like."

I can't tell if this was good or bad news. The doctor seems so wooden in his words, yet he has a sense of urgency. *I wonder if having minimal emotions is required to work in a hospital.* I nod my head in response to his question; *of course I want to see him.*

"We will be back in a few minutes to escort you to his room." With this, the doctor begins to walk away, leaving the nurse behind.

My dad turns to me and whispers, "Is it just me or does this doctor seem too young to even be playing R-rated video games, let alone operate on Corey?"

We both let out a nervous laugh.

Surely, he has gone through years of schooling and clinical rotations. Surely, he has done this procedure a million times and could now do it with his eyes closed. Surely, he would stop the bleeding and we would be leaving the hospital soon. **Right?**

I grab my phone.

"Mrs. Owen, do you and Corey have any children?"

I forgot the nurse was still standing with us. I just started my Google search of "IR procedure" when she asked the question. I slowly look up to meet her gaze while my heart stops beating and my throat grows dry.

I can hear someone answering, "Yes, they have three children." *Am I answering or is it someone else?* I begin to worry that I've lost all power over my mouth when the ringing in my ear comes back, stronger than ever.

"You, or your dad," her eyes bounce back and forth between us both trying to plead with at least one of us, "need to call all three of your children and tell them where you are."

I jump in before anyone else can. "I don't want to bother my children." I hope she can hear in my voice my plea for her to drop it. "It's too soon." *I'm not ready to turn their worlds upside down. I'm not ready to hear the fear in their voices. I'm not ready to try to comfort or reassure them when I haven't even done it for myself yet.*

"Mrs. Owen, your husband is very ill."

Her tone gets lower as she stresses the word 'very.'

"You need to call your children. You will regret it if you don't."

I glance down at my watch. It's just past six in the afternoon. Kristen should be home by now and Thomas would be asking what I've planned for dinner any minute. I imagine Natalie is almost at the hotel. I don't want to think about calling and telling them the news. *What would I say to them? I'm not entirely sure what is going on here.*

More importantly, I can hear Corey whispering, "Not yet."

TOP DOWN DAY

- THREE -

Thomas

I toss my suitcase into the corner of my bedroom; I'll deal with my laundry tomorrow. I head downstairs towards the couch. My stomach growls louder than before, so I check my phone. Still no text messages telling me what time to come over for dinner. My stomach can't hold off much longer; I open the pantry to look for a quick snack. If I eat a small packet of M&Ms I can possibly trick my stomach into thinking it is finally being fed dinner and not totally ruin my appetite.

With no word from my mom, I'm guessing I have time for one round of Fortnite. I turn on the Playstation and plop down on the sofa. I need to work on my skills before Brandon comes home with Natalie and embarrasses me again. *It must be nice to still be in school and have time to put in hours of Fortnite training.* I'll show him how great my work-life balance is; I laugh to myself.

My phone starts buzzing on the kitchen counter. *Now* Mom wants to call me with an update on dinner, right as I'm starting my game. *What perfect timing.* As I approach the counter, I see it's actually a call from my grandpa. *Did Mom invite him over for dinner, too?* I look back at the paused TV screen; I haven't had time for myself all week. I'm sure he'll leave a message telling me what time to be at Mom's house. I hit resume on the game. I would see my grandpa this weekend anyways; we could catch up then. For now, I want to take thirty minutes for myself.

Kristen

The drive home never really feels like home. My parents moved to

Charlotte before my sophomore year of college for my dad's job, and although I know where the closest grocery store is, the area never brings back nostalgic childhood memories. When they told us they were moving, I decided to switch colleges to be near them. I could help them with the move and, then they would be close if I ever needed anything. Plus, after my first year of school, I decided I wanted to pursue nursing and my current school didn't have a nursing program so it really was the icing on the cake. I haven't been back to Pennsylvania since the move; the reminiscing I do every drive home to Charlotte is enough of a visit for me. I never feel inclined enough to visit any more. I can remember so vividly being devastated when my high school friends and I discovered we were all going to different colleges. We promised to be 'friends forever.' Now it's been about five years since I've heard from anyone. *I wonder if Catherine is still dating Louis. He was always such an ass to her.*

Pulling into the neighborhood is when my screen finally illuminates with a call. *It's about time-- someone finally welcomes me home!* The caller reads 'Grandpa' and I'm somewhat surprised he's the first to call me, but I'll take it for what it's worth.

"Hey, Grandpa! I'm pulling..."

Before I can finish my sentence, he interrupts me.

"Kristen, where are you?" His voice sounds somber.

"About to pull into the driveway…"

  I pause trying to pinpoint the reasoning behind his tone.

"I'm a little late because I got held up. Is everything okay?"

  Oh my goodness, my grandma. It has to be my grandma.

"Is Grandma okay?"

Doctors found an aneurysm in her brain a few months ago. They had coiled the aneurysm, and last I heard it had been successful. *Did something change?*

"Yes, *she's* fine. Let me know when you stop the car."

Is he trying to freak me out? My body is getting weaker as the anxiety of the unknown rises over me. I can't remember if I'm pressing on the gas anymore, but I rely on my muscle memory to help me maneuver the car into the empty third garage stall. *At least I'm home first and can claim the extra stall.*

"Okay, I'm parked. What is it?"

"Kristen. I need you to stay calm."

His precautionary words make my heart sink into my stomach and I notice my hands are beginning to shake. *Okay… get to the point already. Dragging this out is doing anything but keeping me calm.*

"Your dad has been admitted to the hospital for internal bleeding."

I listen intently as he continues with current updates on his vitals, blood loss, and units of blood transfused so far. In some sense, I appreciate the figures. He respects my nursing studies enough to tell me the information in a way I could properly digest it. But suddenly, I can't listen anymore. I'm more focused on the faint voice I hear in the background; it's a woman telling him exactly what to say and how to say it. *What is this? Some type of script they had rehearsed?*

"Kristen, are you there? A nurse is standing by if you need to talk to her."

A nurse was standing by... *this must be the voice in the background.*

I'm going to be that nurse someday soon. The nurse giving updates to the families who hold onto every bit of information they receive, trying to make sense of it all. I would soon have to be the nurse willing to talk to distant family members to calmly explain what was going on. I would be in her shoes one day, one day soon. I have been so excited for my career to start, to make a difference in health care, and most importantly, to make my dad proud. I'm the only one who didn't go into business and I think in some ways it made my parents thrilled to have something new. But now, now I'm not sure I want it anymore. The accounting or marketing route seems less complicated, less emotionally

49

draining, more favorable.

Suddenly, a ringing in the distance is all I can hear. Turning my head side-to-side, I try to pinpoint the noise. *Am I making this up? Am I the only one who can hear this?*

I notice the tears starting to drop down my face. I didn't realize I was crying until the wet droplets hit my hand. I go to speak, but nothing comes out. My throat is sewn shut. I can't speak no matter how much I want to. I try to cough to release the tightness, but the cough only brings attention to the pressure in my nose. *I'm beginning to get stuffed up; I must be crying harder than I think.*

"Kristen, the nurse thinks you need to come to the hospital as soon as you can."

My hands are gripping the steering wheel so hard my fingers are numb. *Is this really happening? Why didn't I come home last weekend?*

"I'll be there shortly."

I end the call, not wanting to hear another word. *Does anyone else know? I hope I'm not the last one to find out.*

"Starting your route to Hutchinson Hospital. In one quarter of a mile, take a left on Five Forks Drive."

Thomas

The doorbell rings.

Shit. I pause my game.

"Anyone home?!" shouts out Chris.

I met Chris when I moved into my townhouse about a year ago. He was also a bachelor who gave too much time to his job and didn't have enough time for the dating world...we had a lot in common. He has a six-pack of SweetWater IPAs in his left hand and a family-sized bag of Tortilla chips in his right. *What more could I ask for in a neighbor?*

"Hey, Chris. What's new?"

He was already making his way into my living room when he called back, "Not much. Came over to see if you wanted to hang out for a little."

I glance down at my watch. *Where the hell is my mom, and why hasn't she called yet?*

"Yeah, I can for a little, but I'm heading over to my parents' for dinner tonight. My sister's coming home from college for the weekend."

He throws out an elongated, "Lame" and grabs the other controller.

My phone's buzzing again-- another call from my grandpa.

"Mind if I take this?"

Not giving time for a response, I stand up from the couch staring at the phone screen.

"I'll be right back."

I run up the stairs as I press the green 'accept' button.

"Hey, Grandpa. Do you know what time dinner is tonight? I'm starving."

I guess I should've asked if he was invited first, but I am sure my mom wouldn't care if he and Grandma joined us tonight.

"Thomas, where are you?"

Why did he sound so distant? Did he hear what I just said?

"Um, at my house? I got home about, I don't know, I'd say a couple of hours ago from the airport." I'm confused by the question so my answer comes off jumbled.

"Thomas. Your dad has been admitted to the hospital with internal bleeding. The nurse here…"

I stop him right there.

"What!"

"When?"

"How?"

I feel like I'm in grammar school going over the Five Ws and One H questions necessary to gather basic, *important* information. I still need to ask 'Who, Where, and Why' before assessing the situation, but my grandpa stops me in my tracks.

"I'm sorry Thomas, I know this is a lot to take in."

Yeah, it is!

Stress hormones are rushing through my body, making my body overheat. Adrenaline is pressing in my chest. *Am I angry? What is this feeling?*

"What hospital are you at? I'll leave now."

Why do I feel like I need to punch a wall to release my chest pain?

I turn down the stairs and move towards Chris. I must look as shitty as I feel because Chris immediately let out, "Damn. You okay? Everything alright?" My face flushes more after his comment.

I start to tell him what's going on but my hearing leaves me; all I can hear is a ringing in the background.

"Thomas? You're freaking me out, man."

"I have to, um, go to the hospital."

Even with the words out in the open, it still doesn't sound right.

"What? Why?" *I guess he understands the importance of gathering pertinent information, too.*

"My dad. I better go."

My anger is desperately trying to release from the corner of my eyes. *Don't cry, not here.* I feel the wetness of the tears slide down my cheek, stopping at my jaw trying to hold on before eventually hitting the floor. *I guess crying is better than throwing swings.*

"Let me drive you," Chris says as he guides me out the door. I don't even try to push his offer away. Without him, I'm not sure my feet would keep moving. *I'm losing control of my body.* I open Chris' car door and slowly slide into the passenger seat. Out of routine, I reach for the seat belt and click it in. I'm still in shock, still confused and still unsure of what I'm about to walk into.

"Take a right out of the neighborhood entrance."

I know exactly where the hospital is. I drive past it every Monday on my way to the airport.

When was the last time I called Dad? I try to imagine my Google calendar, refresh my memory of the past few weeks.

Surely, it hasn't been that long. Right?

Dawn

At least he looks like he's sleeping. I was scared the sedation would make him look unconscious or paralyzed, or even dead. *Luckily, to my surprise, he looks peaceful.*

I reach for his hand, trying to interlock the two of ours. *Why is he so cold?* I glance around at all of the IVs attached to him, trying to determine which medication is causing the temperature change. *It's a good thing he's sedated, because he would flip out about being poked and prodded so many times.* The tube down his throat is the hardest piece to look at. It looks so damn uncomfortable; I can barely last thirty seconds before squinting my eyes shut. My eyes fall upon the dried blood lying on the corner of his mouth. The nurses must have forgotten to wash him up. Instinctively, I go to grab a paper towel, but my hands go numb as my brain rationalizes my next steps. *Should I be touching his face? Can I mess any of this equipment up? Would it*

53

hurt him? My eyes well up with tears again as I go through the questions. I begin to wonder how many tears one can shed before there are none left.

There is a soft knock on the door. Swiftly turning to see who is there, I see a brunette nurse standing in the doorway. I've seen her come into the room a few times and add notes to the white board, but I'm not entirely sure who she is. There are too many nurses assisting to keep track of anyone.

"Hi. Mrs, Owen. Your dad wants to speak to you outside."

Her whisper is hard to hear at first. *Maybe she thinks it looks like Corey is sleeping too.*

"Okay, I'll be right out. Thank you."

The ICU unit only allows one visitor at a time. Plus, my dad knows Corey is private about his health. Corey wouldn't want anyone seeing him like this. Especially not the kids.

In a hushed tone, I tell Corey, "I love you. I will be right back," and give his hand a kiss.

Turning the corner, right before I'm about to exit the unit, I nearly collide with a priest. *I pity the poor person in need of a priest's visitation at a hospital.* I almost feel guilty for avoiding eye contact. I scurry around him and go through the doors.

"Dawn" my dad calls out.

"Yes?"

"I called Kristen and Thomas. They're on their way."

We both know the next call is going to be dreadful. We'd have to do some preparation before dialing her number. My hands grip the sides of the chair next to him; I need the support to help guide me into the seat next to him. My tailbone still hurts from these awful chairs.

"I have looked into some flights. The next flight leaves out of Pittsburgh at 7 AM tomorrow and will get her here by 9 AM."

It's so thoughtful of my dad to do the research already. *I'm glad the nurse pushed me to call someone.*

"I guess we should book it."

Playing with my wedding ring helps me think straight.

"Call her first, but then we should book the flight."

"Are you sure you don't want to call her?"

"I can't."

I gulp nervously while vigorously shaking my head.

"I can't talk to any of the kids right now."

Not only because I know it would make me lose any control I still manage to have, but also because I feel like I am personally betraying my husband's wish to keep the kids out of it.

| 7:05 PM |

Natalie

I slide the room key into the slot and push the hotel door open while dragging my suitcase behind me. *Wow, my school upgraded me to a suite!* I open my suitcase and hang up my dress and suit jacket. After I pop my last antibiotic for the day, I grab my backpack and head for the desk.

Last week, my lymph nodes began swelling. I still have three large bumps on my neck and a painful bump under my armpit. My head always feels like it's ready to explode from the pressure and my nose requires a pack of tissues a day. *It'd been inevitable the constant change in seasons in Erie would make me sick. One day it's 56 degrees and sunny, then the next day we'll have a winter storm.* I called my dad the night before finally going to the doctor a few days back. The stress of school and event coordinating was at an all-time high, and not

55

feeling well on top of it sent me over the edge. He kept telling me to calm down and keep moving forward; I was on the homestretch. *He loves that saying, "On the homestretch, Natalie. You can do this."* Anyways, his pep talk and cliché sayings did their magic, and I calmed down enough to book a doctor's appointment.

As I settle into my Advanced Accounting work paper, I hear my phone ring. *I meant to turn it on do not disturb.* I see it's a call from my grandpa. *Did my mom tell him yet about the bleeding?* I wasn't sure if it was still our little secret. *Now that I think of it, I haven't received an update in quite a while.*

On the fourth ring, I still debate allowing it to go to voicemail, but I decide to answer. *I can always use a break from accounting.*

"Hi, Grandpa." My voice is shaky despite my attempt to be nonchalant. *I hate keeping secrets from the family.*

"Natalie, where are you?"

"I just got to my hotel in the city." I don't want to say too much. I still can't tell if he knows or not.

"I need you to sit down. I need to tell you something."

"I already know Grandpa."

"What?"

He pauses trying to process the update.

"You do?"

He seems so surprised. My mom must not have told him she called me earlier.

"Yes. Mom called me earlier this afternoon telling me Dad was in the hospital. She texted me, um, maybe about a few hours ago letting me know the doctors ran a CT scan and found the source of the bleeding."

"Natalie, listen. We need you to come home."

"What? No."

Did he not hear me-- I've already talked to Mom.

"I already asked Mom and she said it wasn't necessary."

My head is shaking side to side, as if my grandpa could see me saying no.

"It isn't looking good, Natalie."

My heart drops, but the drop isn't stopping. It feels like I'm on a roller coaster that never comes back up-- *I'm gonna throw up.* My knees buckle and I flop down on the bed. I don't have enough strength to stand upright anymore.

"Grandpa, you need to call my Mom. I just talked to her. Everything is fine."

I pause before finishing, *"It's nothing serious."*

When was the last time we texted? It wasn't that long ago, right?

"I am at the hospital with your mom," he paused, "and your dad."

I feel the fury slowly coming over me. *How could she not have called me? Why is my grandpa there?* I'm going through the conversation with my mom again. *When did we last talk? Did I miss a call or text from her?*

"Natalie?" I know he isn't sure if I'm still on the line anymore.

"I'm here."

"I've been looking into flights…"

I'm not even listening to him anymore. I cut him off-- "What are the odds? I mean what is the percentage figure he will make it out of this okay?"

My mind is racing. I've always been better with numbers and statistics. I get this from my dad. Everything makes more sense if you can attach a figure to it.

"What? What do you mean?" The confusion in his voice is clear, but I don't

57

care.

"Grandpa, listen. I need the numbers. What are the chances he is going to be okay?"

"I'm, I'm really not sure how to answer that."

"Well, then put on someone who fucking does."

I wince at the disgust in my language; I didn't mean to curse at him. My mom will definitely lecture me for saying a curse word to him, much less the infamous f-bomb.

"Hello, this is Donna. Is this Natalie?"

Who the hell is Donna?! Why are there so many people at the hospital who apparently know more than I do? Why is everyone there but not me?

"What are the chances he is going to be okay? I need a percentage."

"Natalie…"

Her voice is calm and steady. *How are you calm during a situation like this?* Her voice bothers me from the start.

"That's an impossible question to answer. Every situation in a hospital is different. Miracles happen."

This is the most unhelpful Donna in the world. I need to make a mental note to personally find *Donna* when I get there and tell her she needs to work on her calculations.

There's only silence on the line.

"Natalie, I really think you should come home."

"Donna, I really think I need a figure."

"Please" I repeat. I plead.

She sighs before answering, "I would say a 50% chance."

I can take a 50% chance.

Dawn

I can hear my dad arguing on the phone with Natalie. He turns to face me and covers the mouthpiece.

"She wants to drive. She says it'll be faster." He looks exhausted from their conversation. His eyes have lost their sheen and are a tint of red. Even his shoulders stoop lower and his hair is out of place from rubbing his fingers through it so much.

"No way. Tell her no. It's too far."

He turns away and returns to bickering.

Natalie is so stubborn; she always has been. Corey and I always say her stubbornness is why she will be successful. When she wants something, she will get it no matter what anyone else says or thinks. She graduated early from her undergraduate program, despite not coming in with any AP credits, and was going to finish her master's degree soon. She's following her brother's footsteps into the accounting industry. Natalie has watched her brother launch a prosperous career, and I knew she wanted to indulge in the perks of success, too. Somehow, we raised three wonderful kids. All three were on their own pathway to a promising life.

My dad rushes towards me as I drift away in my thoughts.

"Dawn, she isn't listening."

"Ugh. Fine. But tell her she has to drive with someone. She cannot come down alone. No if, ands, or buts."

I don't even need to think about whom she will call. *I know exactly who will take this ten-hour journey with her. I have to call him before she does.*

"Hi, Mrs. Owen. How are you doing?"

Despite me telling him numerous times to call me Dawn, he's always too polite to do so.

"Brandon. Corey is in the hospital."

59

"Natalie told me this afternoon, I am so sorry. How is he doing?"

I don't have time to catch up.

"Natalie needs to come home. She wants to drive, but it's a long trip to do alone. Can you drive with her?"

My sentences feel short and harsh.

"Right now?"

I don't answer; I want to give his brain time to work through the logistics.

"Of course I can. Let me, um, drive to her hotel, I was on my way home but I can turn around."

I hear him pull his car somewhere, switch gears to reverse and eventually back to drive, completely changing his direction.

"Brandon, don't let anything happen to her."

I should've told him to forget it and enjoy his weekend at home, but Natalie needs him. I need him. We all need him.

"She's calling me now."

"Take it. Keep me updated with your ETA."

The phone call ends abruptly and I close my eyes. "God, please get my kids here safely."

This is the first time I find myself praying today. I'm a devoted Christian and right now is the first time I am praying; *and it's for my kids. What is wrong with me?*

- FOUR -

Thomas

As we walk into the hospital, it dawns on me I never received the room number from my grandpa. I shoot him and my mom a text "room number??"

The lady at the front desk seems tired as she looks up from her computer. She's hunched over and if it wasn't for her hand nestled under her ear, I'm not sure her head would stay upright. Our eyes meet as I get closer. Taking in a long sigh beforehand, she asks, "Can I help you?"

"Um, I'm not sure. I'm here to visit my dad but I don't know his room number"

"Do you know what unit?"

Jeez-- I really have no information. My face gets warm from embarrassment in front of this complete stranger and Chris.

"No, but I just sent them a text. I'm sorry."

"What's his name? I can try looking him up in the system."

"Corey Owen."

My voice cracks when I tell her his name. My dad has been in the hospital before, but he never let us visit him. It feels weird and out of place for me to be here now.

"Oh, yes. I see him. Eleventh floor. ICU Unit. Room 1B."

I remember when Kristen had her first clinical rotation in ICU. She told us so many creepy stories at dinner that night; many of them I still am trying

61

to forget. But what stood out the most was when she told us the ordering of the rooms. "Did you know the room numbers actually signify the urgency of the patient? The first rooms are for those in the most serious conditions." I remember thinking it made logical sense and couldn't figure out why it surprised her so much.

I swear I can hear her telling us about it right now. Fuck. He's in room 1.

Kristen

This elevator is going so slow. I'm astounded at how full it is when I first enter the elevator on the ground floor. By the time I reach the eleventh floor, it has made 6 different stops. *Why is the ICU unit always so high in hospitals? Doesn't it make sense to make it the second floor so families can see their critical loved ones right away?*

The doors creep open, and I'm surprised at the number of faces that turn to look at me when I step off the elevator. I assume many families are waiting for others to join them in the dark waiting room. It's almost as if I can hear someone saying, "closer, almost there, a few more steps" as I walk around the corner trying to find my mom. My body knows where to go without thinking.

I see my brother first. His eyes look puffy. *Is he crying?* I can't remember the last time I ever saw him cry- or really if I ever have. *Who are all of these people sitting with them?* It takes my brain a second to recognize Marianne. *What is she doing here?* Then I try to make out who is next to my brother, but my brain can't make sense of his face.

My brother shoots up from his chair to come give me a hug. He isn't saying a word. On top of the shock of his welled-up eyes, I can't believe he is hugging me right now. He only hugs me when I ask for one.

"Who is that next to you" I whisper in his ear.

"Oh, it's Chris, my neighbor. He drove me here."

I wish someone drove me here. I could barely see the road, my eyes were so foggy from tears.

"I better be heading out," I hear the now-known Chris announce. Thomas heads over to walk him out and thank him for coming. I look back at the others in the room. Marianne seems so put together. I don't know her very well, but there is something about her right now that brings comfort to the room. Her eyes seem light and she cracks a soft smile when her eyes meet mine. She doesn't say anything, but she doesn't need to. I know she is there to support us, with whatever we need. Which reminds me, I never made it inside to let Oakley out. *He has surely had an accident in the house by now.*

I make my way over to Marianne to tell her but my feet stop in front of my mother. She doesn't seem phased by my presence. I lean in, "Mom?" I ask. No response. I sit down next to her and grab her hand. She feels cold, but then again she is always cold. She appears surprised by my touch and jolts back a little. "Hi sweetie." Her eyes seem tender and the circles under them seem darker. I can tell she is being strong for us, or at least *trying* to be strong for us.

"I'm going to let you all be together. I'll take care of the house and Oakley. Nothing to worry about back home."

We all look up at Marianne. She has always been such a good neighbor to my parents. Despite the fifteen-year age gap between her and my mom, Marianne was always there for her, for us.

"Call me if you need anything." She's looking firmly at my mom when she says it. We all know it will take a lot for my mom to ask for help. Before anyone can respond, a nurse appears in the hallway. *I wonder if this is the nurse I heard during my phone call with my grandpa.*

"They are starting the procedure. The doctor will come out with an update once the procedure is finished."

I didn't know about a procedure. I have questions and I need answers, but my mom looks too tired to talk.

Natalie

"Hello?"

"It's gotten worse, Brandon. I have to go home" My mind is still running rapidly.

"I know, your mom called me."

> *You have got to be kidding me. She could call him and not me? She made my grandpa call me-- so much for being her confidant.*

"What's the plan? I can meet you at your hotel." Brandon knows I already would have a plan in motion.

"No, no. My hotel is out of the way and I don't want to sit here waiting for you. I want to meet right off exit 23. It's in between us both and it won't delay us."

"I think there's a Wal-Mart right there. I can park in the parking lot."

Brandon never thinks things through. This tends to be one of my biggest pet peeves about him. He lives too much in the spur of the moment; he doesn't think five steps ahead like I tend to do. But maybe that is why we work so well together-- he flies by the seat of his pants and I overplan; almost to the point of sucking the fun out of everything.

"Who knows how long we'll be there. Do you really want to come back to your car being towed from a Wal-Mart parking lot?" I am being snooty and I know it. I don't know why I do this. He's only trying to help, but I can't help it as the sarcasm rolls off my tongue.

"Okay, I'm sorry. What do you think?" He's so timid now. *Did I make him feel like this? Am I always this rude when I panic?*

"I'm going to call Casey. Her parents live two miles off the exit and I'm sure she is home for the weekend already."

I hang up and give her a call as I frantically pack my suitcase back up. I'm running between the bathroom and the closet trying to gather everything as I listen to the unanswered rings.

"Hey Nat!" she finally yells.

There's a ton of background noise. I can barely hear her over the loud music and countless people yelling around her. *Where is she?*

"Casey, are you home?"

That's a dumb question. Obviously she isn't. Unless her parents were suddenly into throwing ragers.

"No, I'm at a friend's apartment. Why? What's up!"

"Um, It's a long story…"

I let my voice trail off so I have time to take a deep breath before going on.

"But I have to drive home."

I can almost hear my heart beat now.

"My dad's in the hospital."

I hate saying the truth out loud, no longer able to avoid the reality of it all. My vision begins to blur as the tears fill my eyes. *You can't lose it Natalie, not yet.*

"What! Is everything okay?"

Her voice gets sharper and I can tell her buzz is starting to wear off with the sobering news.

"Look, I was wondering if I could park Brandon's car at your parents. He's making the drive home with me."

"Of course--I can come with too. Tell me what I can do. I'm only 20 minutes from my parents; let me know when you're close."

She's such a good friend. She always wants to help, but truthfully I don't want to see her. I don't want to see anyone. Not even Brandon. I know I will lose it, and I hate that side of me.

"No, there is nothing you can do."

"Let me know when you're close. I want to give you a hug."

A hug isn't going to solve anything, or even make me feel better. It will simply waste time.

"I will. Talk soon."

As I hang up the phone, I already have decided I will tell her when I'm five minutes away, knowing it won't give her enough time to race home. I'll tell her I completely forgot and I got tied up with the drive. *I can't see her. I won't know what to say to avoid breaking down.*

Flashbacks of recent phone calls with my dad come to mind during my drive to meet Brandon. It's been almost three months since I was last home. My friends and I went to Punta Cana for our last college spring break. Our last get away before the real world would hit. I saved up enough money to pay for the trip for myself and Brandon. A few years ago I promised myself I would stop asking my parents for money. I worked three jobs in college, but it was worth it.

I remember sitting in my friend's kitchen talking to his parents before we left for the Pittsburgh airport.

"I feel guilty for not going home this spring break."

My mom didn't seem thrilled when I told her my plans in February. I knew she missed me and really just wanted me to come home for the week.

"Why, sweetie? Your parents understand you have been working so hard. You'll be home soon enough. Go enjoy yourself!"

Mrs. DeLeo made me feel better for the moment. *My parents did understand, right?* She made me feel like my guilt was unnecessary, but now I'm wondering if I was on to something after all.

I have to get away from my thoughts or this drive alone will send me into an anxiety attack. I need to call someone. I look through my contacts and land on my grandmother. I haven't heard from her yet and I'm sure she is struggling not to call us.

She picks up on the first ring. "Natalie, where are you?"

Why does everyone keep asking that!

I ignore her question. "Any update on Dad?"

"Nothing yet."

Her voice cracks, trying to keep herself together and not fall apart to me.

"I have been praying so hard, Natalie, I really have."

She stretches out the word really, almost trying to emphasize it in an attempt to convince me.

I know she is praying; she doesn't need to convince me. She's always been good about saying her rosary, especially for others. My throat and chest tighten with each prayer she says over the phone. The hole in my heart grows deeper with every additional prayer to St. Jude. We're one of hundreds, thousands, millions praying to St. Jude for a miracle. *How can prayers make me feel so empty? So small?* I don't mention any of this to her. She keeps praying while I listen in silence. It feels like hours before she stops, but at least it is numbing my emotions.

After what seems to be her hundredth 'Glory Be,' the silence takes over the call. She doesn't know what to say anymore; all of the prayers have been exhausted but I still have about forty-five minutes until my exit. The eeriness of the line is starting to get to me. Images of a hospital bed, my family sitting in a waiting room, my dad being rushed to surgery start filling my mind. No longer in control of my vision, I watch as the scenes play out. Tears falling from my sister's eyes, doctors trying to explain what is going on, I squeeze my eyes shut trying to make it all stop.

"This can't be happening! It can't."

I let go.

Panic sets in and fear rises to meet my tears, patiently waiting to be released. I let out every emotion I'd been so desperately trying to hold in. Each sob makes it harder to breathe. Each breath I take feels like I'm getting the wind knocked out of me. *This isn't how it's supposed to be. We're not the family this stuff happens to.* The road isn't as clear anymore. My grandma keeps saying, "Natalie, I need you to breathe," and "Natalie, how much farther until you meet Brandon." But I can't answer her. I can't talk, I can't think, I can't do anything but press my right foot down on the gas pedal. As hard as I can.

Out of nowhere, the bright green exit sign is glaring at me. *I am minutes away from Brandon. I need to pull myself together, and I can't do that talking to my grandma anymore.* As I end the phone call, she promises one last time that she won't stop praying.

Off the exit, waiting at a red light, my phone dings with a text message from Brandon. "Picked up the essentials. Red Bull, tissues, and a bottle of Equate Stay Awake caffeine pills. Get here safely. I love you." *This is going to be a long car ride; hopefully by the time I get there he's feeling better.* I'm grateful to soon get to be in the passenger seat, to focus on anything besides driving.

Before pulling into Casey's driveway, I make one last plea. "God, please let us get there safely," I whisper as I look down at the clock and notice that it's almost ten o'clock at night. It physically hurts to cry now, but I manage to whisper one last thing. "Let him be okay... please let him be okay."

| 10:49 PM |

Thomas

The waiting room is starting to empty as families are deciding to get a good night's sleep before returning in the morning. I scan the room. People have glassiness over their eyes, staring off into the distance. I wonder if the majority of us are sleeping with our eyes open. My grandpa seems so weak in the corner. I can't tell if it's because he's so tired, or if he knows this scene too well. He is in charge of informing my dad and my mom's family of the news. I can't imagine the toll this role is taking on his body and mind. *I would hate to have to retell the same story to multiple people as the devastation sets in on the other line.* I think about all of the whimpering tears he must be hearing.

68

Thank goodness he is here with us. My grandparents moved from Colorado to South Carolina about a year ago. It was difficult for them to leave the state they loved so dearly, but both agreed it was time to leave the mountains and move to warmer weather. They are about a twenty-minute drive from our house now. *Funny how things tend to work out the way they do.*

I swear my mom hasn't moved a millimeter in the past half-hour. She is as still as possible. It's almost as if she thinks any movement will screw something up. I turn to face my sister. She hasn't stopped crying since she got here. I tried comforting her earlier, but it didn't seem to help so I brought her tissues and moved my seat. *Sometimes you have to let them cry it out.*

We all seem so distant right now. We haven't spoken a word since the nurse last came out.

The opening of the door is such a faint, but distinctive noise. Everyone still in the waiting room turns their neck so fast to see if it's their turn to get an update. I wonder how many of us will have a crick when it's all done and over with. My mom stands up. *She must recognize the nurse who signals us over.*

"The surgeon and ICU doctor will be out shortly."

Not quite the update we're looking for, but at least we know we are close. Shortly after, the doors open to reveal a man in a white coat. His age shows under his eyes, but the blackness of his hair hides any evidence of being older than forty.

"The Owen family?"

No one says a word, but I assume someone shook his or her head because he continues.

"We found the source of the bleeding. It appears he had a rupture in his gastric artery. I have to be honest…"

His pause lingers throughout the room.

"This is one of the biggest ruptures I've seen. Are you sure he wasn't on any abnormal medication? Blood thinners?"

"No" my mom blurts out. "He had foot surgery a little bit ago, that's why he has the cast on his foot. He was on pain medication, and aspirin, for that surgery. But that's it."

The doctor's eyes turn to the ceiling, trying to connect the dots.

"Full-strength aspirin, I guess." She adds slowly.

Why did she correct herself? The doctor writes down the additional information and looks back up at us.

"We stopped the bleeding for now. It's definitely looking better than before the surgery. And, truthfully, if all remains good, this procedure may have just saved your husband's life."

The air feels lighter; the energy feels stronger. The hope is slowly rising in the room. My grandpa smiles directly at my mom, who finally seems present again. He grabs his phone and heads for the hallway. I assume he is going to update the family on the news of stopping the bleeding.

"Corey will be allowed to have visitors shortly. But I must warn you, you must be calm. We want to ensure *he* stays calm, but I think hearing from you all might help him. Give him strength."

The excitement in the room pushes us all to stand up and pass along hugs. *It finally feels like we are in this together now; we can do this together. We can see the light at the end of the tunnel again.*

Dawn

The embrace of Kristen and Thomas gives me strength. I can feel my body regaining energy with each hug. The door opens again, but this time it's a face I don't recognize. I assume it's a doctor for another family, but then he comes over and slams into the chair next to us. *Can't he see that we're in the middle of celebrating the first good news of the night?*

"Dawn Owen?" he grunts.

I answer, confused, while glancing over to my kids; "Yes?"

"I am the ICU doctor. I have been monitoring your husband."

"Oh, hello! Did you hear the good news? The surgeon came out and told us they stopped the bleeding!"

My voice is giddy with excitement. *We needed this.*

"Look. I was supposed to leave at 7 PM tonight. I should be with my family right now, but I'm here and it's almost midnight."

Squinting my eyes, I try to figure out if he's being serious, if he's really saying this to *us* right now. *Look doctor, we also have had a shitty night so I'm going to need you to take your pity party somewhere else.* I can't help the amount of distaste on my facial expression to this new doctor.

"We aren't out of the woods, Mrs. Owen. Your husband still has a long way to go."

Even as he pauses, he refuses to look up to meet my eyes.

"We aren't sure of any organ damage as a result of the prolonged bleeding."

If he's going to be in a bad mood about getting home late, that's fine, but don't bring us down. Not after we received good news-- very good news, for the first time today. He reaches for his breast pocket to grab a business card and, suddenly, it turns into 52-card pick up.

"Damn it!"

All wide-eyed, we watch him lunge towards the floor. Kristen leans down to help him pick up some of the fallen cards while the rest of our eyes go back and forth between each other's faces trying to make sense of what exactly is going on.

"I'm sorry. Here's a business card."

He hands one over as he continues to pick up the rest.

"Call me if you need anything. I will be back in the morning to check on him and our staff will be closely monitoring him tonight."

Ha! As if I would call you! You're already bothered enough having to stay late. I can't imagine adding on to your inconvenience. Blood is boiling and I can't help but think, *this is your job, isn't it?*

"He's not out of the woods, Mrs. Owen. I want to be clear on that."

His eyes look so fatigued. The redness of his eyes brings attention to the dryness and intensity of the day. *He must be sleep deprived, or delusional, at the least.* Once he finally leaves, we all look at each other confused on what just happened. The energy is rocked, but it isn't gone.

Natalie

The car ride has been pretty quiet so far. No music playing, and, between the two of us, I'd guess less than seven words have been exchanged. I wish I could talk to Brandon, see what he is thinking, but I know I need to remain silent. The moment I open my mouth, there is a chance I won't be able to stop. The fear of what may be unleashed overcomes me and I remain hush. Plus, the silence helps me feel numb. The quietness allows me to take a step further away from reality, and I prefer this feeling over opening up.

My phone rings and I hit accept before even looking at who it is. The call automatically connects through Bluetooth.

"How's the drive?" It's Thomas.

"Any update?"

The irritation builds up inside of me and my voice sounds snarky. I have sent everyone individual text messages asking for updates six times and no one has answered. *I understand it was my decision to move to Erie, but at least answer me!*

"The doctors found the source of the bleeding and fixed it."

I didn't realize I had been holding my breath in, but suddenly it's releasing from my lungs as I hear the good news.

"It's looking super hopeful here!"

Did we make a big deal out of nothing? Are we driving down here for nothing?

The irritation inside of me redirects from my family to myself.

What am I thinking? It isn't going to be for nothing. I will be able to talk to my dad and tell him to never scare me like this again. Tell my mom she needs to call me next time shit hits the fan, and not pass the job off to my grandpa. Plus, if nothing else, it's a free trip home.

"But I guess we aren't out of the woods," Thomas adds.

With my eyebrows furrowed, I look over to Brandon. *What does that saying even mean right now? Does he get what Thomas is saying?* Before I can even make sense of it, Thomas continues to talk.

"The nurses will be out shortly to guide us to his room to say goodnight. We wanted you to be on the phone so he could hear your voice. The doctor thinks hearing us will help him stay strong."

What-- I'm so not ready to do this! The thought of having to speak starts all of my fear to slowly rise inside of me, taking over each limb, and my eyes begin to get fuzzy again. Brandon reaches for my hand. *I swear he always knows what I'm thinking before I say it out loud.*

"Let me talk to Mom," I mutter.

I can hear the phone shuffling between hands.

"Yes?" Her voice sounds raspy. I imagine she's worn out, but not admitting that to anyone.

"How are you?"

"The doctors seem hopeful."

She didn't answer my question.

73

"How are you?" I repeat.

"Hanging in there, sweetie. What is your ETA?"

She's trying to change the subject, but I won't keep pushing at it.

"Between 6 and 6:30 AM."

There's a pause in our conversation; I vaguely listen to, who I assume to be the nurses, come out and signal it's time to my family.

"The nurses are coming out. Stay on the phone."

There is a lot of mumbling on the other line. All I can make out is Kristen sniffle. *Pull it together, Kristen. We need to sound hopeful; let him know we're right here waiting for him to push through.* Then I hear a door open; the creak so subtle but in a quiet hospital it's easy to make out. More mumbling. *What is going on?* I look over to Brandon to see if he can make sense of it. His face puzzled, trying to focus on making out their words. *Are they talking to Dad? Am I supposed to be talking?* I can't help but wonder if I missed my signal, and I'm missing my opportunity to tell my Dad how I'm rushing home, how I'm so hopeful, how he can't give up, how I'm so sorry.

"I can't hear anything!" I blurt out.

My tears feel harder, more dense. Each one slides down my face faster than the tears before.

"I can't hear anything!" I scream again.

Why are they doing this to me? I feel so isolated in this car. I want my family. I want to be in that room with my dad. *Fuck Erie. Fuck my master's degree. I am never leaving home again.*

"Natalie, did you want to say anything? I'm putting the phone up to Dad's ear now."

Yes; I have been trying to freaking talk, I think to myself. *Calm down, he needs you to calm down.*

I clear my throat and wipe away the evidence of tears on my cheeks and lips. "Oh, Dad…" I don't know what I'm saying, it's all spilling out without me even thinking through my words, but at this moment I don't care. I just want him to hear me, hear my voice. I want him to know I'm on my way home, and I'll never leave again. I promise.

Kristen

No one has a clue what she is saying over the phone, but all of the sudden a small amount of blood starts dripping out of his mouth, his stomach rises, and his eyelids slowly try to flutter. *Is he trying to cough? Is he trying to answer her?*

My dad has always been so close to Natalie. She always had to show us up with some new job or another 4.0 GPA. They comment every week about some Wall Street Journal article. *Of course he is trying to answer her.*

The nurses ask us to leave the room for a moment while they make sure he is okay. Thomas is telling Natalie goodbye, but leaves out the part about what happened when she began talking to Dad. *I'm guessing to try to protect her.* She would be devastated if she thought she caused him any more pain. *He obviously can hear us. But why did her voice cause such a change in his demeanor?*

I look over at my mom watching every move of the nurses inside his room. As Thomas heads down the hallway to take a moment for himself, I walk towards my mom. She must feel my presence because she turns to face me.

"I think you and Thomas should go home. Drop Grandpa off and go sleep at Thomas' house. We have a long day ahead of us and I need you all well-rested so I can lean on you when I need a break tomorrow."

I know she isn't going to leave his side, but I can't deny how tired I'm getting. I had completely forgotten Grandpa was still sitting outside the waiting room. *I wonder why he didn't want to see Dad.*

Through a head nod and a squeeze of my eyes, I signal my agreement to my mom and hug her goodnight. Thomas reappears from the hallway, joining us again. My mom informs him of the plan and he kisses her cheek goodbye.

The elevator ride down to the first floor is silent. No one saying a word. I send Lindsey a quick text, "Can I call you in thirty minutes?" I know she is probably already home, and I need someone to talk to about all of this; someone besides my family.

As we climb into the car, a text comes through from Natalie. "Keep me updated tomorrow. Please." *I know I need to be better with the updates, but she doesn't realize I know just as little as she does.* I text back "Okay. See you tomorrow. Dad will be excited to see you."

Thomas

As we exit Dad's room, something isn't sitting right in my stomach. *Why did that happen when he heard Natalie's voice?* I think back to hearing people say that those suffering wait until everyone they love has had a chance to say goodbye. *Is this that moment, did I just unknowingly say goodbye to my dad one final time? Why didn't I say more? Do more? Give one last hug, tell one last joke? He isn't going to make it, is he?*

My head begins to spin and I can't see clearly anymore. *Is this what it feels like to have your world come crashing down?* I watch the fear come over Kristen's face and I instantly realize I need to pull it together; I need to be strong for my sisters, my mom, and the rest of our family. They need to feed off of my energy, my strength.

I decide to take a minute for myself; I need to let out this deep feeling of rage or sadness or whatever is messing up my head.

I make my way down a long white hallway, no end in sight. I think about calling someone to talk to, *but who do you call on a Friday night? How can I deliver this news? Will I ruin their night?* Without letting my mind wander anymore, I decide to call a college buddy. The next five unanswered rings drag on for an eternity. *Seriously? How can Andrew not answer in the moment I need him most?* Pissed off, I end the call and scan through my contacts. I land on another college friend and try again.

"Hey man how's it going?" Matt asks with such ease.

Little does he know.

My words are all over the place in my brain and I don't know if I'm making any sense. "Um, I don't know man."

The energy shifts and I can tell he picks up on the severity of the call.

"What's going on, man? Talk to me!" His voice sounds anxiously fearful.

"It's my dad; he's in the hospital and it's not looking good."

As I finish the sentence, it's as if someone opened up the Hoover Dam and let the Colorado River flow. I have officially lost it. Strategically taking each breath in order to avoid anyone from hearing me, I cry. I let it all out. I hold each breath in as long as possible while the tears pour out. In this dark corner, I realize the doctor was hopeful, wasn't he? *What am I doing? Have I given up hope on my dad?* My stomach flips into a knot and the rising guilt makes me feel like I'm about to vomit.

"What is going on?!" Matt keeps repeating over the phone.

Shit, I'm still on the phone! How long has he been listening to me whimper and lose my shit? What else has he been saying? I gather my thoughts, wipe away the tears, and tell him I have to go. *Get yourself together!*

I take one last deep breath, and remind myself that Dad is going to be fine, he is going to pull through this. *Be strong for your sisters and mom! Stop giving up hope!*

Part II

SATURDAY

MARCH 23RD

TOP DOWN DAY

- FIVE -

Dawn

His monitor starts to beep again; the noise is ear-piercing. I wake up immediately. I hadn't realized how tired I was, and I certainly hadn't meant to fall asleep, but this recliner in his room is quite an upgrade from the chairs in the waiting room.

Nurses and doctors start piling in and reading off his vitals. The noise of the charts flipping is all I can focus on. Pages swishing drowns out the frenzy in their voices as they call out numbers on his monitors.

"Give him two more bags of blood" one calls out.

Why are they still giving him blood? I thought the bleeding stopped last night? I don't want to ask any questions because I don't want to be kicked out of the room again. I look down at my phone. Natalie texted me nearly twenty minutes ago letting me know she hit Virginia. I'm not sure I'm ready to see her; face another one of my child's uneasy hearts. Plus, she never did well seeing people sick in the hospital. My mind drifts back to last spring.

Kristen had gotten terribly sick on the tail end of our Alaskan cruise. The doctor on board was convinced it was strep and kept telling her to get tons of sleep, so she did. Once we made it home, she still was feeling ill. She couldn't hold down any food, not even her dad's famous barbeque chicken. I knew something wasn't right, I suppose it was the mother instinct setting in. We went to our local doctor. She ran multiple tests, speculated several causes, and had a strong inclination Kristen had Rocky Mountain spotted fever. This didn't make much sense to me, but what did I know; I'm not a doctor. When Kristen started to develop a rash, I knew the medication prescribed wasn't working. I was fed up with not getting an answer, so I took her to the emergency room, praying someone would finally take us

81

seriously. Upon arrival, it was confirmed that Kristen had, in fact, turned septic and was severely dehydrated. The doctors finally confirmed she had Cytomegalovirus (CMV), basically mono, with a compromised immune system. She spent 13 days in the hospital, and eight of those days in the ICU. The fear in Corey and I as we watched our grown daughter barely have enough strength to chew food was eye-opening. Natalie visited a few times, but struggled every time. She hated seeing her twin sister that way and often times her eyes remained glued to the floor during her visits. It was hard on all of us to see our healthy 22-year-old daughter so sick.

How is Natalie going to be when she finally makes it here? I can feel my heavy eyes begin to fall shut. I guess we'll just have to wait and see.

| 4:38 AM |

Natalie

"Do you think you could drive for an hour or so?" Brandon breaks the silence with the question.

"Oh yeah. I'm wide-awake."

I pause to take the last sip of the Red Bull in the cup holder.

"Pull off here and we can switch off."

As he puts the car in park, he turns to me and says, "Don't go crazy with the speed, Natalie. Getting pulled over will only slow us down." I roll my eyes. *He is always lecturing me on my speed.* I begin to wonder if that's why he never lets me drive places.

I watch Brandon's eyes start to close and his head start to fall back. I guess I didn't realize how tired he really is until now as I watch him doze off so quickly. Glancing down at the clock, I notice it is 4:38 AM. My heart aches as I wonder how Mom is doing. *I bet she's exhausted, but trying to stay strong for everyone; especially Dad.* I let my mind wander to Kristen. It's a not so well-kept secret that my dad has a huge soft spot for her; I mean huge. Kristen

82

has always been very different from Thomas and I, and I think my dad relates to her in some ways. He is always easier on her than he is with me, I mean really easier, and at times it's hard for me to accept. I am constantly trying to impress my dad, whether it be graduating early, receiving another scholarship, or finishing the CPA exams in 4 months. Yet, Kristen simply finds a new murder mystery show and my dad is impressed. My cheeks wet with tears, I realize how petty I'm being. I know my dad is proud of me, and Kristen, and Thomas. *Why am I always comparing myself to them?*

I see the lights before I hear the sirens. **Fuck.**

Brandon wakes up immediately; pulled out of a deep sleep with the loud noises surrounding us. He doesn't scold me; he simply adjusts his position to sit up and calmly watches me pull over.

It feels like it's been hours until the police officer finally exits his car and makes his way over to mine. The car window is already rolled down bringing cool air into the car, and my hands calmly placed on the steering wheel. His footsteps, slow but loud. The bright light shining directly into my eyes makes it hard to see. *Is your flashlight really necessary?* I blink my eyes a few times until I can finally make out his face. Every muscle in his face is tense; his lips pursed enough to create fine lines around his mouth. The heat of his eyes peering down at me make my hands tremor.

"Ma'am, did you know you were going 85 in a 55?"

His accent is clearly southern.

"No. I apologize, officer." I'm being short. I'm too exhausted to even try to get out of this ticket right now. I just want to get back on the road, and make up for the time I'm losing now.

"License and registration please."

I shuffle through my wallet and grab my driver's license. Turning towards Brandon, I wait for him to get the registration from the glove compartment in front of him. The sound of papers being pushed around when he can't find it makes my frustration begin to grow. *How hard is it to find this piece of paper?* Brandon finally grabs the registration and hands it to the officer. Not without me giving him a snarky look first. The officer takes the paperwork and goes back to his car. *Great, more time wasted.* I fall back into my seat, shoulders hanging low.

I hear Brandon mutter, "What is that look for?"

"I didn't realize how hard it is to grab a piece of paper."

"Natalie, I'm sorry," he sighs, "I never looked for it before in your car."

I throw my head back and turn the other way. I know he's right. I'm wrong. *Why am I lashing out at him?* I only have myself to blame for setting us behind, yet I'm taking it all out on him. *Perfect.*

Watching the officer in the rear view mirror, he opens his car door and slowly makes his way back to my car.

"Ma'am whose car is this?"

Right when I think I've caught my breath, tears begin to well up in my eyes.

I can't look up at the officer. My chin falls to my chest, and I feel the warmth of Brandon's hand covering my hand. He still cares about me even when I'm being a total brat to him; *I don't deserve him.*

"It's my dad's." I whisper so softly I wonder if he can hear me.

"Where are you off to tonight, ma'am?"

The question makes the corner of my lips curl down. Slouching even more, I clear my throat to answer.

"My dad's in the hospital."

Letting the words set in, I take a pause before I finish answering his question, "I'm headed there now."

My head is still facing my lap, but I can hear the officer slowly move backward. Without looking up, I know he is heading back to his car. *More time lost-- great.*

Shortly after, he comes back and hands me a piece of paper saying, "Ma'am,

I'm only giving you a warning tonight. But you need to slow down; focus on getting there safely."

Shocked, I look up to face him. His face less tense; his eyes softer than before. He gives me a nod and a half-smile. *I guess people down south really are nicer.*

"I hope your dad is okay."

Yeah, me too.

|5:15 AM|

Dawn

I haven't slept much. Maybe two thirty-minute increments. I toss and turn, hoping I'll wake up to a different story.

I check the clock on the wall; it's a quarter after five. *Natalie must be getting close.* I send her a text, "about an hour out?" *I hope she and Brandon were able to take turns driving and sleeping. I need everyone to be well-rested. This is going to be a long day ahead of us.*

One of the doctors late last night, or maybe it was early this morning, informed me that Corey had lost a lot of blood flow to some of his organs. His kidney and liver were the main discussion points. They would need to run tests later in the day to see which, if any, have been severely impacted. I remind myself to ask more questions today. I strategize; I will ask my questions during the day and be quiet during the night. This way I can ensure that I can sleep in the same room as him every night we will be here.

My phone pings and I quietly turn my phone to silent mode. *I guess it doesn't matter; he won't wake up with all of the sedation he's been given.* My heart aches at the thought of it.

Natalie's text reads, "Yes, be there soon. Any update?"

My fingers paralyzed over the phone's keyboard; I think of how to respond back. *Do I tell her the number of people funneling into the room every hour, still pricking him, still giving him blood, still sedating him?* I decide to send back a simpler, "No." I understand there is nothing I can say or do to get her here sooner, so I sit back into the familiar chair and pull the blanket around me tighter. Trying to curl up and get comfortable, I allow myself to rest my eyes once more.

Forty-five minutes later, I wake up and immediately check for Natalie's location. I can see on Find My Friends that she is only fifteen minutes away, yet she isn't moving. I zoom into the map, trying to figure out where she is. *Where could she possibly be?* I copy her address into Google. The image of a Dunkin Donuts storefront is returned from my search.

Why would she stop? She is so close! Doesn't she want to see her dad immediately? See me? I can't stop myself from feeling hurt.

| 6:02 AM |

Natalie

As we pull into Dunkin Donuts, I jump out of the car as fast as possible.

"Wait, up!" Brandon yells out to me.

"Hurry, we have to make this fast! We are so close."

I want to surprise my mom with a coffee and bagel. I know she prefers Dunkin over any other coffee locations. It really did take everything inside of me to stop here instead of Starbucks. If I know my mom, she hasn't taken a moment to eat anything, and I also know she won't be able to refuse a sesame bagel with loaded cream cheese.

With the warm to-go bag in my lap, I text my mom, "Pulling into the parking lot." *Finally. We made it.* She writes back right away, "ok. I will meet you by front desk." I'm glad she is meeting me at the reception area. Hospitals freak me out, and I hate talking to strangers about why I'm there

86

and who I'm visiting.

Brandon switches the gear and I watch the lite up 'D' switch to 'P'. The car door feels heavy as I hoist myself out of the car, holding onto the door for support. My legs start to feel weak as we walk through the parking lot. *I should've eaten something on the way over.* My stomach is starting to fill with cramps. *Is it the Red Bull I drank on an empty stomach, or are my nerves to blame for my discomfort?*

I see my mom before she sees me. *She looks like shit.* Her hair is greasy and she's tightly wrapped in a white, grimy blanket. I'm guessing she convinced someone to lend her a hospital blanket while she slept in the room with Dad. *My dad always likes his room cold.* I turn my head and squint my eyes, trying to take it all in. Somehow she looks smaller, weaker, more fragile. I stop in my tracks as I take in the sight. *Am I ready to do this?* Brandon must sense my hesitation because he turns to grab my hand and whispers, "I'm right here with you." I roll my eyes and pull my hand away.

I have no idea why I'm doing this, absolutely none. I love this man. I'm thankful he is with me, but I can't help my walls from sprouting up around my heart. *I need to protect myself in all of this. It's not strong enough to let anyone in right now.*

The automatic doors open and my mom turns towards me. The pain is obvious in her eyes; it runs deep within her. She starts to cry as soon as we catch one another's eyes. I'm guessing she hasn't done much crying until now because each sob is blaring. She is always trying to be too strong, but she knows that front wouldn't work with me.

"Oh, sweetie. I am so glad you made it."

She kisses me on the cheek and pulls me in for a hug. I nestle my head into her shoulder, and watch as my tears leave a wet mark on her shirt. As we part, Brandon gives her a hug and she shows us to the elevator.

"Natalie, the nurses said they would give you access to his room to see him. I know he would love to see you."

I take a moment before softly answering, "I'm not sure I can yet."

87

I am telling the truth. I'm not sure I can handle the sight yet; making the reality of it all really set in. When the elevator stops on the eleventh floor, I'm surprised to be greeted by empty seats, no one else is waiting to see loved ones. Then I see the sign reading, "Visitor Hours: between 10 AM – 5 PM." *How am I able to see him right now? Why do we have special privileges?*

We find three seats near the window, and settle in. My mom holds small talk with us about the traffic and the weather driving here as I hand her the sesame bagel. I decide to leave out the part about being pulled over for now; I can't see how that information will help the situation right now. Time is passing, and I know she is patiently waiting for me to change my mind about seeing Dad.

"I really think you should come in with me. It will be okay. I'll be right by your side."

What is with everyone telling me they will be right by my side? I don't need anyone right by my side. I need my dad to stop bleeding and get out of this damn hospital.

"And… if it's too much, we can step out."

"I'm not sure."

The thought of seeing the strongest person in my life so helpless leaves me with an uneasy feeling and sweaty palms.

"Natalie, the doctors have told us he can hear us when we talk to him. He can feel our presence."

She's going to guilt me into it.

"It lets him know we care."

He knows I care-- doesn't he?

"Okay, okay. Fine." I see her face light up and a smile grows on her face.

"But if I don't like it, I'm leaving immediately," I add. I want to be clear so I don't ruin any expectations she may have for me.

"Of course."

She takes my hand and we buzz into the ICU unit together. The walk to his room feels gloomy and lengthy. Eyes to the floor, I try to focus on the specks on the ground, counting each one. I remember the mistake of looking up and seeing other sick patients the last time I was here visiting Kristen. *That memory feels so far away now.*

My mom pauses outside of Room 1B; my gut knows this is his room. She doesn't say a word, but she takes my hand again as we step inside together.

I lose my breath as chills run through my body ending at the tips of my fingers. My body is paralyzed in terror of accidentally tripping and pulling a wire loose. *Who is this person in the hospital bed?* His fingers look blue, and I know his skin is cold without even touching him. *This is not my dad; this can't be my dad.* This stranger has a tube down his throat and IVs *everywhere.* The man lying here is so swollen, I can barely make out his eyes. I can't distinguish his neck from his face anymore.

I search around the room. I can't figure out where the noise is coming from. It's growing louder and louder. I want to ask my mom if she can hear the ringing, but words can't be formed. Realizing I'm still holding my breath, I notice my vision getting hazy. My legs are getting shaky. My throat tightening and my chest closing in on me.

I look back at my dad. *How can my biggest protector in life look so hopeless lying on this bed?* Fear is setting in and I can't stop it from traveling through every inch of my body. *Does he really feel my presence?* Letting go of the breath I'd been holding in since I entered the room, I mumble, "I can't do this. I'm sorry, I'm *so* sorry.."

My mom comes chasing out of the room behind me. "Honey, it's okay. Come back."

She thinks I'm saying sorry to her. I had completely forgotten she was even in the room with me and Dad.

| 8:54 AM |

Kristen

The phone ringing is ear piercing. Jolting up straight, I feel disoriented. *Where am I? What day is it?*

My brain begins to connect the dots. Disappointment setting in, I was hoping last night would turn out to be a dream, better yet, a nightmare. Before I fell asleep last night, I prayed I wouldn't wake up in Thomas' house. I prayed I would be at my parent's waking up to bacon crackling and coffee brewing. I prayed I would walk downstairs, Oakley by my side, and see my dad drinking coffee at the kitchen table. Yet, here I am, waking up to the loudest phone call ever, reminding me that my dad is still in critical condition.

"Thomas! Your phone."

I throw a pillow at his face to abruptly wake him up. *We must have fallen asleep on his couch.* Thomas rubs his eyes open, looking around the room before grabbing his phone. *I wonder if he had a similar prayer last night.* I can't believe I slept as hard as I did. *How am I able to sleep so peacefully knowing my dad is sedated and intubated?* I try shaking the guilt from my conscience.

"Okay, we'll head over now. Yep, okay."

I look around his new place while he is busy on the phone. *He is such an adult now.* He bought this place a few months ago. Scanning his living room full of art work and home decor, I realize I'm not ready to have my own house with my own bills anytime soon.

"See you soon." Thomas is wrapping up his phone call now.

"That was Natalie. She and Brandon made it this morning. I guess they went to Mom's house to get some sleep, but...um, before they made it back Mom called telling them to turn back around. Dad is going into emergency surgery or something."

I don't have the desire to find out more; plus I don't think he really knows any more than that. I imagine the next steps before we moved. Us in the car, rushing into the hospital, rejoining my mother in the waiting room, no one knowing what to say. Without much thought, we hurriedly slip on our shoes and head for his car. I haven't uttered a word since I woke Thomas up this morning and I decide to keep it this way during our drive. In the midst of silence, having plenty of time to think, I realize I haven't brushed my teeth or combed my hair. None of my daily maintenance routines seem important anymore. I rest my elbow on the edge of the window and prop my head up against my fist, staring out at the passing rows of trees while lost in my thoughts.

As we enter the hospital, I see Brandon first. He looks so out of place picking at his nail beds. I'm sure he feels unsure if he should be here or not. My eyes fall upon Natalie next. Her skin pale, and her nose cracking from using too many tissues and not enough lotion. I remember Mom telling me she came down with a cold last week. Yet, I know she isn't just sick from a cold. She doesn't do well with hospitals. The smell of the sanitizer and unsettling feeling of a hospital would be enough to make her feel unwell. I remember feeling guilty every time she came to visit me last year when I developed CMV. I tried to tell her she could call for updates instead of coming in; I was too weak to even try to have a conversation. She would just sit in the corner, not say much and barely look at me. I don't think she wanted to see how swollen and red my body had gotten from septic shock. She has the same pale skin now; her face and hunched body looks like she could vomit at any moment.

I go over and give them both a tight hug. Natalie doesn't say anything, just holds me and then sits back into her chair. Brandon makes nervous small talk about their drive and asks how nursing school is going for me. *He is trying so hard; I wonder if Natalie notices.* Then, my grandparents enter the hospital. *I wonder who called them.* Grandma looks like she hasn't stopped crying in months, her nose is raw and her eyes swollen from too many tears. Grandpa still has the uneasy look he wore yesterday plastered on his face. Neither of them are the most comforting sights.

Finally, my mom emerges from the elevator. We all face her.

91

"They just took him back." She goes to grab a glass of water, but her shaky hands drop the cup. A tear sheds from her eye and falls onto her cheek. *She's exhausted.*

"What happened?" Natalie finally speaks.

"I just saw him. What happened?" She keeps going on as her voice grows with intensity.

"I don't know." *My mom sounds so weak.*

"Well, you have to know. You were the only one in the room. What the hell happened?"

Why is she raising her voice? Natalie and my mom never fight. I look at Brandon, who looks like he wants to simply disappear now. Earlier, he tried to hold her hand but she pulled away. *Are they having relationship problems?*

"Natalie, knock it off. If she says she doesn't know, she doesn't know," Thomas hisses back at her.

My grandma catches my eye; her fingers frantically rubbing her rosary beads. I can tell she wants to cry during the argument, but is trying desperately to hold it in and not say anything. I imagine my grandpa lecturing her this morning about the importance of staying strong for Mom; keeping quiet. It must break her heart watching this all unfold; not being able to protect my mom.

"Did the doctors say what the surgery was for, Mom?" I try asking calmly, hoping I won't upset anyone since it's obvious everyone is on edge.

"The bleeding started again."

Her pause is weighing on all of us as we anxiously wait for her to finish.

"After weighing out the options, the doctors decided they had to open him up. It is a more invasive procedure, but I guess the risk is necessary if they have any chance of stopping the bleed for good."

The bleeding came back… how is this possible? Where is the doctor who said the IR procedure worked? He told us last night he saved my dad's life! He reassured us that he was more stable.

"He isn't out of the woods" keeps replaying in my mind. *How could we have been so naïve to believe him?*

Natalie

I know I'm not helping the situation by lashing out, and Thomas definitely doesn't have a problem reminding me of it.

This isn't like me to talk to my mom this way. Why am I disguising my fear and sadness with irritation? Especially with her and Brandon. I'm certainly not angry with my mom; she has to know that. With everyone crowding around in the waiting room, I have no space to talk to her alone, to tell her I'm sorry. I reach for my phone and shoot her a text message. "I'm sorry. I am tired and I know you are too." *However, there is a more important question I need answered.* Dad and Mom always tend to leave us kids in the dark with medical information, but I won't let her leave me behind this time around.

I follow up the previous text with, "Be honest. Did the doctors say this is life or death?"

Dawn

The text message pops up on my screen instantly. *Why is Natalie sending me a text from across the room?* My heart physically hurts when I read her text message.

I know she is tired. I know she doesn't mean to lash out. I know this is hard for everyone, especially Corey.

Another ding.

A distant ringing noise appears in the background as I read her next message. Every limb is paralyzed after her message sinks in. *Did the doctors say anything of that sorts? Do I have a response to this question?* I start to type out an answer, an honest answer, and then delete it. Looking around the room,

I see the pain so evident on everyone's faces. *We have to be strong for each other. I have to be strong for everyone. I can't let them begin to lose hope-- even if I am.* I send back, "No. We aren't there."

|1:14 PM|

Thomas

It's been nearly two hours with no update. My mind needs a distraction.

"I'm going to grab something to eat from the cafeteria downstairs. Does anyone want anything?"

Brandon looks up at me. I had an inclination he would do just about anything to leave the waiting room, so it doesn't surprise me when he stands up to join me on my food quest. Kristen and Grandpa yell out their orders. I look over at Mom, her stare completely blank, and I wonder if she even hears me.

"Mom, want anything to eat?"

"No, I'm okay." She squeezes her eyes shut and slowly reopens them, bringing her back to reality.

I had already decided to grab her an apple, but I figured I would give her the option. Right before we turn to go towards the cafeteria, I hear a door push open. My instincts tell me it's finally time for an update. I hear a nurse call out, "Owen family" before I even turn around.

Thank God I didn't head for the cafeteria a second earlier.

As we all gather around, the nurse explains that the doctor would be out shortly with an update. The surgery has ended and he would be able to provide more information on how it went and next steps. Anxiety is lingering in the air as we wait, knowing our update is close by. I don't want to look up, for fear of meeting anyone's eyes. *I have to be put together. If I see the pain in their eyes, even for a millisecond, I know I will lose it.*

The doctor comes out, rubbing his hands. He seems as nervous as we all are.

"The surgery is finished. We opened Corey's abdominal cavity, creating about a nine-inch incision."

Holy shit-- nine inches? That seems large! Scanning everyone else's faces for similar shock, I notice no accompanying open mouths or wide eyes. No one else seems phased by the comment. *Maybe this is a normal incision?*

"Quite frankly, the blood came pouring out. We took out about a liter of blood clots."

My heart sinks and my lungs hold in the air, refusing to let it out. *How did it get this bad?*

"The stomach was lined with ulcers."

Feel free to spare some details; can't you tell the pain your words carry? Torn between vomiting or getting up to get fresh air, the doctor keeps going.

"With the massive amount of blood, everything is completely swollen. The stomach became so enlarged, the sac around the spleen ruptured. So, unfortunately, I had no choice but to remove the spleen."

My mom's intake of breath is so loud, it's heart wrenching to hear. The doctor looks at her and pauses before continuing.

"We have a new fast-acting gel; it's an injectable hydrogel bandage. It's essentially a *magic gel*."

I make a mental note of this *magic gel; I'm sure Google has some type of information about it.*

"I poured this over his wounds and sources of bleeding. It's really our *last resort* to try to contain the bleeding."

Vocal sobbing is taking over every inch of the room. Kristen can't help but wail in response to his words. The doctor's jaw twitches; I imagine how uncomfortable it must feel being the person responsible for delivering such life-altering news. *I wonder if he finds himself sugarcoating updates in attempts to alleviate some pain, since he knows damn well he can't prevent it.*

"Due to his swelling, I could only pack the wound; I wasn't able to close the incision. I have him on the schedule to go into surgery tomorrow morning to check the progress of the gel and, hopefully, close the wound."

They didn't even close him up? Dad will be mortified knowing we will see him with his stomach exposed. The doctor is turning his head, trying to look at us all.

Trying to reassure us, he continues, "Listen, he is better off now than he was before the surgery. For that reason, I think the surgery was a success. In the morning, however, we may need to remove his appendix and take a look at his kidneys."

Are you kidding me?

"During surgery, I noticed his kidneys don't seem to be fully functioning. I notified the nurses to start him on dialysis when he returns to his room. We also may need to consider the likelihood of removing his stomach tomorrow."

You can live without your stomach?! I can't even begin to imagine how this is possible.

"I've done this procedure only one other time in my career. It isn't the most ideal form of living, but it is manageable. I know this is a ton of information thrown your way. Do you have any questions I can try to answer now?"

Would it be acceptable to ask him to repeat everything he just said? There is no way I heard that all correctly.

"Is he going to survive all of this?"

I can't make out who asked the question. We all are thinking about it, but I never would've dared to be the one to vocalize it. Silence fills the room. *Why is he taking so long to answer?*

"I am honestly not sure. Truthfully, this is the first case I've ever seen like this."

I recognize this is a tough question for a doctor to answer, and I respect his honesty.

"But, if he does make it out of this, it's going to be a long journey and you all need to be prepared for it. During surgery, we had to induce him into a light coma to guarantee his safety during the procedure and potentially for his future. I'm worried about his kidneys not producing urine and the long-term effects of his organs from losing blood."

He's talking about his brain. I overheard my mom telling my grandpa the nurses were going to re-evaluate the Glasgow Coma Scale because the ICU doctors were nervous about his brain functionality. My mom mentioned the possibility of Dad waking up and being a completely different person, but never shared with us about his low Glasgow score. *I hate how she withholds certain information from us. I wish she realized it doesn't protect us, it blindsides us.*

"Well, if that's all the questions for now. I'll notify the nurses to grab you when Corey is ready for visitors."

Although we're clinging onto his every word, without question, the word 'visitors' stings. *We aren't simply 'visitors' we're his damn family!*

| 3:12 PM |

<u>Kristen</u>

We are now waiting on the eleventh floor's waiting room. *Jeez, today has been consumed with a whole lot of waiting around.*

A text from Lindsey glows up my screen. "Thinking of you and your family." I told her yesterday about my dad. It feels nice having other people to talk to about my feelings besides my family. However, I feel guilty for telling outsiders. It doesn't seem like anyone else is texting their friends. Well, besides my grandpa, of course. He's so good about quietly leaving the room and updating family members as we find out more. I'm surprised we

97

haven't received a text message from our dad's sister. She looks up to her brother so much, and we all know it. *I can only imagine what the updates are doing to her.*

"I wonder if you should notify your professors" my mom utters.

I haven't even thought about school. All of the homework due on Monday suddenly comes to mind. If I am going to be allowed to turn in my assignments late, I would have to give my professors enough notice. *What do I even say?*

I begin to draft an email to my professors. *Did I need to email each one individually or is a group message okay?*

"Dear Dr. Murphy,

I wanted to make you aware of a family emergency that has arisen over the past 24 hours.

My dad has been admitted into the hospital with internal bleeding. The doctors seem hopeful about the recent surgery, but have assured us the journey is going to be long. I want to be by my family's side until he comes out of the coma.

I hope my dedication to my schoolwork has been evident this semester. I do not plan on deliberately missing any assignments or exams, but I was wondering if I could keep you updated on my situation in case I were to need an extension.

I completely understand if this is not possible, and I am willing to accept any ramifications which may follow.

Kristen Owen"

This draft seems very formal, but I send it anyway. I update Lindsey on the possibility of me missing some classes next week, and ask her for the study notes for Thursday's test. *I'm sure I'll make it back for that.* Plus, even if I'm not going to make it, I could use the distraction.

I hear Natalie updating my mom on her call to her boss and the director of her M.B.A program.

"I spoke with Dr. Ash and Dr. Brown. Both told me to do whatever I need to do for my family and they would manage without me. Thankfully, there are no more events left in the semester so my workload will be minimal. My professors reassured me my grades are sufficient to miss a few weeks of school."

She always seems so much older than me, even though she isn't.

"I can't believe we still aren't allowed to go back," groaned Thomas "it's been almost two hours since the last update."

"I really wonder if you should all go home. Go eat some dinner and come back later tonight." *Mom's concerned we aren't sleeping enough, when she should really be worrying about herself.*

"No, I'll stay with you." *I don't want to go anywhere.*

I look at my brother and sister. Both appear drained. Natalie and Brandon both look at each other and exchange exhausted looks. I keep forgetting they are going on about 36 hours of not sleeping. *I can't imagine what their body must feel like right now.* I can barely keep a straight thought, and I got seven hours of sleep last night.

"Seriously, go home. Get some rest and come back tonight. It will be better for all of us if we rest up."

My grandpa is the first to answer. "I think Mom and I might take the offer. Call us if you need anything, Dawn."

Why do I keep forgetting my grandparents are here? I watch them hug and kiss her goodbye. They are trying so hard to be resilient for her.

"You need to eat dinner too." Natalie had a point. I don't remember seeing

99

my mom eat since Marianne brought dinner for us last night.

"Go cook something for dinner and bring me back some of it. It will help me more if you go home. I promise."

We all moan. None of us have acquired my Mom's cooking skills.

Brandon proudly sits up and adds, "I can make baked ziti for everyone and bring some back for you, Mrs. Owen." His addition makes him feel like he has a purpose for being here again.

"Perfect," my mom responds smiling "But you must get some sleep before cooking. Natalie, could you grab me some clean clothes too?"

Natalie takes down the clothing items my mom needs, and then we head to the elevator.

As the four of us enter into the elevator, the familiar silence returns. "I still have hope. I think he's going to make it out of this." Natalie spoke softly, but she seems confident in her assessment. Brandon reaches for her hand, and this time she lets him hold her. "I think so, too," both Thomas and Brandon respond. I look Natalie in the eyes and only manage to whisper, "I hope you're right."

- SIX -

Dawn

About forty-five minutes after everyone leaves, a nurse comes looking for me. She guides me down the halls, eventually leading me to Corey's dark room.

I am taken aback by the number of nurses in his room. The nurse in the corner looks up from the machine in front of her. *She must be in charge of dialysis.* I know this machine well, as Corey's mother had to have it when she was suffering from Lupus. Corey always told me how hard it was on their family knowing this machine was the only thing keeping her alive. *We aren't there yet with Corey; I just know it.*

Before sitting back into the familiar recliner, I turn to face Corey. I am thankful for the blanket covering his open wound. *He looks better than before the surgery.* His face has more color and the swelling seems to have gone down. My spirits begin to rise and I want to let everyone know. I send out a quick text to the kids and my dad, "made it back to the room. looking better than before. all good signs!"

My eyes feel heavy as I hit send.

As I am getting settled, I hear the head nurse direct the other nurse in the room to write down his score of 4.

When I wake up, I will ask her what this means. I'm only going to rest my eyes for a few minutes.

I wake up to a nurse screaming, "We keep chasing the numbers here! We need to get more blood!"

She doesn't seem to notice I'm in the room. The alarm in her voice rises as

101

she runs around the room checking different monitors. *Did they never get him stabilized? How long was I sleeping?* Three more nurses appear in the room. Rubbing my eyes, I check the time-- it is almost four in the afternoon. I notice a text from Natalie; she sent it about forty-five minutes ago.

"How's Dad?"

She is going to get suspicious if I don't answer her.

"sorry it is crazy busy in his room. he is about the same."

Almost immediately she pings back, "Why so busy, still not stable??"

She always has a sense when something is wrong. "not really. but close."

Is that even true?

Natalie

By the time we finally make it home, we have already drawn up our plan. Thomas and Brandon will head to the store while Kristen and I prepare a bag for Mom.

When the boys leave, Kristen looks at me and says, "I can do this by myself. Why don't you go lay down for a little?"

I don't even have the will to tell her no. My head feels foggy from my lack of sleep.

"Thank you. It'll be short, I promise."

My eyes are killing me. I try rubbing them to relieve the extreme dryness and itchiness. I head to my room and look in my suitcase. *Where is my bathroom bag?* Pulling every last piece of clothing out of my suitcase, rummaging through my backpack, still nothing appears. *Shit. I must have left it in the hotel room.* I stare at my empty bathroom. I have no contacts, no glasses, no antibiotics, and no toothbrush. *I'm going to be a pleasant person to be around.*

I'll go to CVS after I lay down for thirty minutes. My head feels heavy and I can feel my body craving sleep. Right before my head hits the pillow, I hear my phone. *Finally, an update on Dad.*

"sorry it is crazy busy in his room. he is about the same."

Did I read that right? I rub my eyes again trying to clear my vision. Once I re-read the message, I feel a burst of energy throughout my entire body. Any tiredness I felt before is completely gone and the urge to go to bed has disappeared. I quickly send a response and wait eagerly for her to answer. Biting my fingernails and picking my skin to create hangnails. *What I really want to do is call her.* I want to hear my mom's voice-- then I can determine how bad the situation is or isn't, and if she's bullshitting me. *Tone is hard to capture in a text message.*

"not really. but close."

My gut is urging me that she's hiding information. *She isn't telling us the full truth to try to protect us. I hate when she does this shit; it makes me paranoid.* The garage door opening scares me upright. Positioned right below my room, the movement of the door going up shakes my bed. *Thomas. Kristen. I need to see them, tell them.* I race downstairs, skipping every other step.

Kristen is spraying down the pan while Thomas comes in with his hands full with grocery bags. Thomas cracks a joke, so typical, and it sends Kristen off into a laughing spree. *Maybe I should wait to say anything until I get a clearer response from Mom.* They both finally seem relaxed, and for a moment, the trauma isn't consuming every part of their brain. Detouring my original plan, I head to the door to help Brandon get the last bags. He pulls me aside.

"I'm sorry if I'm doing something wrong."

I want to lean in and kiss him. I want to tell him he isn't doing anything wrong. I want to tell him I'm sorry for being so rude. I keep locking 'I'm sorry' in a box and never opening it up for anyone. But before I can say or do anything, I hear a phone ringing in the kitchen. I know it's mine, even though all of our phones have the same generic ring, *I just know it's mine.*

Thomas

I watch the color in her face disappear while she talks on the phone with Mom. She's never looked this weak before. She is so similar to my Mom-- definitely a hard-ass; always trying to stay strong, even when no one asks them to. Something in the corner of my eye catches my attention. Brandon is holding Kristen. I imagine Kristen realizes just how serious it really is since she has a background in all of this medical shit. She hasn't been able to keep any emotions in these past two days. I have to turn away; I hate seeing Kristen cry. She's usually trying to comfort everyone else. But she can't anymore; she is scared of losing her best friend. I'm glad Brandon is here to help comfort people, because I'm too exhausted and busy trying to hold in my own tears to try to console someone else right now.

"We have to go pick up Mom. They're transferring Dad."

Natalie is already halfway out the door when she finishes her sentence.

"Grandma and Grandpa will meet us at the new hospital."

We all look around, confused, but we quickly follow her when she yells out, "Hurry up!"

On the way to the hospital, Natalie catches us all up on her phone call.

"The hospital is running low on his blood type, I guess. He has gone through thirty-one or so units of blood, but still needs more. And the surgeon told Mom he's running out of ideas on how to stop the bleeding. He's hopeful the main hospital will have more options."

Kristen speaks up, "Their staff is better trained in trauma and the hospital has more resources. Makes sense."

I keep forgetting she's gone through clinical rotations in the different hospitals in town, so she understands each hospital's specialty.

"You guys still have hope, right?"

Natalie shoots us all a look when she asks her question. Her body language appears irritated, yet weak. I can tell she wants us all to be on the same page before we enter the hospital. Looking at Kristen, Natalie pushes her head forward implying she's waiting for her response.

Brandon is the first to answer, "Of course we do."

Peeking in my rear view mirror, I watch him take her hand. I'm surprised she didn't pull away. *She always acts like she doesn't need others to comfort her.*

Kristen whispers to me, "What do you think?"

"I'm hopeful," I mutter before contemplating how I really feel.

I want to tell Kristen I'm not entirely sure. I want to tell her how I'm uncertain of what the next hours will hold for us. However, I need to reassure both girls, because I know they need it. I also don't want to know what will happen if Natalie thinks I'm losing hope.

I know it's not right, but the night before keeps fucking with my head. I did have hope though-- right?

| 6:36 PM |

<u>Kristen</u>

Mom is sitting in the waiting room on the eleventh floor. Foot tapping, hands running through her hair, she seems frustrated, but who can blame her. God only knows the last time she had more than thirty minutes of sleep.

"I told my parents to meet us at the main hospital. I don't know *what* is taking so long."

She gets up and starts pacing near the door. I watch Natalie go over to her, whispering something in her ear, and sure enough she visibly calms down. *Natalie is always good at talking Mom down from the ledge.*

Finally, a nurse appears in the doorway. "The Owen family. You can say

105

your goodbyes now."

Goodbyes? Why would she use **that** *word? Of all words,* **goodbye** *is the one she chooses?* I know I'm overthinking.

"The pilot is on his way over now. It'll be about twenty minutes till he starts his flight to the main hospital."

I look at Natalie. *She didn't mention Dad was being air-flighted to the new hospital.* I can tell she is just as surprised as I am. Thomas and I make it to the room first. His stomach isn't covered anymore. The incision is wide open; the large cut down his stomach exposes his insides for everyone to see. Before I can even sort out my emotions, I turn to Natalie and yell, "Stop!" *She will not want to see this. If Natalie sees Dad like this she will lose her hope and she is the only one with unaltered hope.*

Natalie stops in the middle of the hallway, feet stuck to the ground. She knows I am protecting her from seeing something. She trusts my judgment and doesn't come any closer.

"Tell him I love him and *I'll see him soon*," she whispers.

Wiping tears from her eyes, Natalie turns around and heads back towards the waiting room. Passing beside her is the pilot. He takes one look at my dad and says, "He isn't going to fit."

What! What does he mean he isn't going to fit! Not knowing what to do, the nurses exchange surprised, yet concerned, facial expressions. I slowly turn towards my dad. It is the first time I really *look* at him. His stomach is so inflamed, it's hard to see his face. Not just his stomach, but his arms and legs are significantly bigger as well. Leaving no room between his arm and hand, the distinction of his wrist is no longer there. The swelling really has gotten bad. *How did I miss this before?* He's retaining fluids from all of the blood the nurses have pumped into him.

The pilot repeats, "He isn't going to fit. His stomach is way too swollen. The helicopter only has 15 inches of clearance. With all of those monitors and IVs, I am telling you he will not fit."

I hear my mom let out a sob from behind me. Emotions running high, I whip my head back to face her. She's pacing back and forth again muttering, "You have to be kidding me."

The ICU doctor must have heard the commotion because he enters the crowd from the hallway. "What's going on?"

The pilot starts again, "He isn't going to fit. I'm not having my team bring him to the roof and waste time."

The ICU doctor signals to the nurses to stop. This is when I notice the nurses have found a tape measure and are trying to determine the height of his stomach while he's lying on his back. I shiver thinking how embarrassed my dad would be if he saw all these strangers measuring his stomach.

"What should we do?" the nurses ask frantically.

"Take him by ambulance. Transfer him from the flight stretcher back to his bed, and get him downstairs fast."

The ICU doctor sounds so calm in his orders. He looks at us now with piercing eyes.

"Traffic won't be bad on a Saturday. The ambulance will get him to the main hospital just as fast as the helicopter."

Everyone is moving quickly, barely allowing time to think. The nurses are transferring my dad to a new stretcher and reorganizing his monitors. The EMTs come rushing through the doors, barking to the nurses that an ambulance is waiting outside exit 3.

"Goodbye, Dad. See you in a few minutes." Thomas lets out, barely able to hold back his tears.

"I love you, honey. See you shortly." Mom's voice sounds so shaken.

Turning to look directly at the ICU doctor before meeting Thomas and my mom in the hallway, I ask him one final question. "I need you to be honest. Is he going to make this transfer?"

I need to know so I can prepare myself.

107

"Yes, he will make the transfer," he turns his head to avoid eye contact as he finishes his sentence, "but making it through the night is a different story."

- SEVEN -

Dawn

Leaving the hospital parking lot, we hear ambulance sirens exiting the area too. *Corey's in that ambulance, I can feel it.*

We're stuck in unusual Charlotte traffic, and I can see the ambulance three cars ahead of us, also stuck in traffic. *Move the hell out of the way!* The medians on the road make it impossible for the ambulance to get around the cars ahead. Our car hushed in silence, I only hear occasional breathing. All watching the same scene, no one knows if we should cry or get out of the car to direct traffic ourselves. *Please God, get him there safely.* The traffic begins to clear and we lose sight of the ambulance. I actually begin rejoicing when I can't hear the sirens anymore. *He's getting closer. He's going to make the transfer.*

Once we arrive at the main hospital, Thomas drops me and the girls at the main entrance while he and Brandon go park the car. Natalie sets the pace as we run to the front desk to check if the ambulance has arrived yet. Before Kristen catches up to us, I hear Natalie whisper, "You still think Dad will make it out of this right?"

"I do," I answer without giving my response much thought.

It's after this question that I begin to realize I haven't really thought about the other option if he didn't make it through this. I've been running through the motions, listening to the updates, waiting during the surgeries, but I wasn't really focusing on the other option of only two possible endings. *He can't die. What would we do without him?* I shake the thoughts out of my head and continue towards the front desk.

We are directed to the twelfth floor: the trauma ICU unit. We take our seats and begin to wait like we've been doing all day long.

109

| 9:41 PM |

Dawn

It's been almost an hour and no one has updated us or even come out to tell me he's made it into his room safely. The waiting room is dimly lit. There are three families besides us waiting; I don't have the energy to make up their stories in my head to pass the time. Thomas turned on Impractical Jokers when we got here. The television seems to help numb his pain, but I can't stand listening to them laugh. *I can't imagine ever laughing again if Corey doesn't make it out of this.* My dad has fallen asleep in the chair next to my mom. I doubt either of them have gotten much sleep over the weekend. My mom keeps peeking at me; I know she's worried about me but she doesn't realize how much her looks are actually stressing me out. Natalie is sleeping on Brandon's shoulder. She's wrapped up in the flannel he gave her when we first got here. I laugh when my eyes set on Brandon, his head completely fallen back, not resting on anything. *His neck is really going to hurt when he wakes up.* I look over to my youngest, the illumination of Kristen's phone is so bright. She has been playing the same game on her phone since Friday. I wish I could play Candy Crush, but I'm haunted by the memory of it. *Did I miss something on Friday when I was too busy playing it? What kind of terrible wife sits and plays a game on her phone while her husband is in pain?* I delete the app off of my phone and go to check if I can enter his room yet.

The new hospital means new nurses who don't yet realize how often I will bug them to get into his room.

| 10:17 PM |

Natalie

"Natalie, wake up!"

Thomas is nudging my shoulder so aggressively I nearly fall out of my chair. Disoriented, I almost pass out from standing up from my chair so quickly.

"Shit!" I hit my hip hard when I bang it on the stand next to me. *Why the hell is it so dark in here?!*

As I'm racing to Thomas, he calls out, "Wake everyone up. They have a room waiting for us."

I'm blinking hard now to regain focus in my eyes. *I need to get new contacts tomorrow.*

We all walk through the ICU doors together. Yesterday, only four people were allowed into the unit at a time. Now my grandparents, Kristen, Thomas, Brandon, and I are all allowed in together. I'm thankful for the exception to the rule, but I feel an uneasiness come over me when I think about the purpose behind it.

As the nurse leads us to the private rooms, I see a disheveled teenager sitting outside one of the doors. She sounds like she is hyperventilating from crying so hard. I can only imagine the news she's just been given. I want to go sit by her, not necessarily hold her; just sit next to her.

When the nurse opens the door to our private room, my mom is waiting for us. I didn't realize while I was asleep in the waiting room, she came back here before any of us. She is crying. No, she is sobbing. *Why?* I haven't seen her cry this hard the whole weekend. *What does she know that we don't?* She won't even look up at us. I have to look away; it hurts too much to watch her like this. *If she isn't containing herself anymore, how are any of us supposed to?* Before we fully walk in, I feel Brandon tug me back.

"Are you sure I should come in? I don't mind waiting outside."

Taking a deep breath before answering, "I need you."

The walls around my heart slowly begin crumbling. It's the first time I'm finally admitting it. *I need Brandon more than he knows; more than I have been showing, that's for sure.* Brandon has to be there when all of the walls decide to

111

finally fall. *I can't do this alone.*

We all pick a chair and sit down. The doctor places his hand on my Mom's shoulder. "I'm going to leave you alone with your family."

How long has my mom been in here alone?

"We'll begin the surgery in about two hours. We need to sterilize the room first. If you need me, the nurses know how to reach me."

He takes a long, deep breath before finishing his thoughts, "I'm sorry."

Why is he sorry? He doesn't leave time to go over any questions we have like the previous doctor. *Why isn't he explaining what is going on?* He simply walks out of the room with all of my burning questions unanswered.

"I don't…"

Her downcast eyes finally rise up, not turning away anymore, I see not only her sadness but her heartbreak.

"I'm not sure…" Mom tries to speak, but nothing is coming out. She buries her head into her hands.

My grandma tries to stop her pain by reassuring her, "Dawn, it's okay. We're here when you're ready."

Looking up again, she takes a breath to gather her strength. "The doctors need to go back into the wound to try to stop the bleeding again. The gel hasn't…"

She keeps stumbling over her words every time her voice cracks. It's hard to listen to her try to speak; she's trying desperately to remain calm.

"The gel hasn't worked."

She takes a moment to wipe away the mascara that's running under her eyes.

"Dad's gone into hypovolemic shock and he isn't stable enough to move to the operating room. The surgeon has agreed to perform emergency surgery in his room. It's apparent his kidneys and liver are failing."

Her eyes dart to the floor as she ends her sentence. Every word tugging at her heart.

"The surgery will allow the doctors to get a better assessment of his organs and make the decision about putting him back on dialysis."

I can't move; my fingers tucked into a tightly gripped fist, my entire body is tense. My throat burning dry, I am at a complete loss for words. I can't stop the tears from completely flowing out of my eyes, but it doesn't stop the stinging. Snot is building up on my upper lip when I realize there aren't any tissue boxes in the room. *Whose brilliant idea was it to not place tissues in the private rooms where apparently shitty news is delivered.* Brandon goes to search for tissues when I rub my nose on his flannel.

Kristen brings her knees up to her chest. She is rocking back and forth with every sob she lets out. I think back to when we were younger; she has always been more sensitive than me. Thomas and I would always poke fun at how easily she would cry. I can't imagine how shattered her world is right now. My grandma doesn't try to hold her tears in anymore. She is crying into my grandpa's shoulder, who still looks completely shocked. This isn't how it's supposed to be. *Your son-in-law should be in the private room listening to news about your state; not the other way around.* Thomas is pacing the room.

My mom grabs Thomas' hand with tears welling in her eyes, and whispers, "It is okay to cry."

This is all he needs to hear. Slowly finding his seat, he puts his face into his hands and lets it all out.

There is a knock on the door. *Who now? How can it get any worse?*

A man in a black outfit slowly shuffles into the room. His clerical collar gives him away before I notice the bible in his hand. *Has my mom given up hope? Why else would she ask a priest to join us?*

Dawn

What is a priest doing here? This has to be a mistake. Who called him?

Thomas

Looking so obviously out of place, the unknown priest asks, "The Owen family?"

"Yes! God Bless you for coming," my grandmother responds.

Searching for a chair, he continues to ask, "I hear you're having a tough weekend."

I nearly laugh out loud at his comment. *Good guess! What gave it away-- the fact that we're spending our weekend in a hospital or the loud sobs coming from my sisters? You are quite observant.* As I sit trying to manage a balancing act of composure between rage and sadness, he comes in with this comment. *What, is this his first night on the job?*

"I have come to help guide you to peace in the days going forward and answer any questions you may have."

No one answers. I'm waiting for the crickets. *I wonder if everyone is feeling as uneasy as I am right now.* His voice sounds too upbeat and I don't think talking to a stranger about my emotions will solve anything right now. I'm getting ready to ask him to leave when I hear my mom say, "Father, what do you recommend we do right now?"

|10:51 PM|

Kristen

Why does this priest seem so nervous? His voice makes him seem almost excited; honestly, it's creeping me out. Turning away, my attention falls onto the slightly different colored paint covering a fresh drywall patch. *I wonder if someone*

114

punched a hole in the wall.

I listen to him answer my mom, "I think you need to walk into your husband's room and tell him everything you have ever wanted to tell him. Tell him what you wish you'd said in last year's Christmas card or thank him for the vacation you took for granted. Don't leave anything left unsaid. Once you've done this, I think you need to pray to let God's will be done."

Maneuvering in his chair, he faces us kids and further explains, "You know, life is like a snow globe, and God is the only one who can shake it when it's time to watch the snowflakes fall."

What… What the actual hell is he talking about? My brain is not in the mood to untangle some symbolized life lesson. *I need to go talk to my dad.* I definitely haven't been the most dedicated Catholic recently, but I know for certain that I don't want to regret anything. The words of the ICU doctor telling me the night isn't looking favorable is *ringing* in the back of my mind. *I need to go now, before anything happens.*

Natalie

I go to church weekly, I say my prayers every night, I thank God for the food on my plate, but I don't think this man has any right to tell me when it's time for my family to give up hope. *We need to focus our prayers on his health, on saving him, on making deals if only God saves him.*

I simply can't believe my ears when I hear my grandpa say, "Thank you Father. We needed to hear this."

This isn't your decision! I want this priest to leave. I *need* this priest to leave. *No one is giving up on him. We aren't giving up hope.*

My sister and brother leave the room. I assume they are going to see my dad, but they better not be saying goodbye. *This isn't the end; it can't be. Dad can't think we're losing hope. He **is** going to make it out of this. Sure, it will be a long journey, but he is going to be okay!*

115

Thomas

Kristen stands up, and I join her outside of the room.

"I need to go talk to him," she says frantically.

Quietly, I respond, "Me too."

As we both enter the room, nurses are running around everywhere, trying to sanitize the area and stabilize his vitals.

Kristen reaches for his hand. *She's braver than I am, but I'm glad he can feel our touch.* Her blue eyes begin to silently weep. She wants to be strong for him. After wiping her face and clearing her throat, she begins to speak.

"Dad, it's Kristen and Thomas here."

Nervously, she shifts her weight from one foot to the other before continuing.

"We love you so much and we hope,"

I can hear the sound of the air slowly filling her lungs as she takes a deep breath.

"we hope you know that."

He knows that right? Why wouldn't he? I look up at the nurses circling around us. They seem unphased, so unbothered by our words. *I wish we had a moment to ourselves.*

"I want you to know whatever you,"

Her pause makes the sentence awkward.

"or God-- decide, know we will be okay."

Will we though? Looking up to her, I see the same doubt in her eyes.

"We just want you to be happy."

Her voice is shaking while she twists the ring on her left index finger.

Seeing how uncomfortable she looks, I chime in, "Dad, if this world is too painful, don't stay for us."

I can't believe I'm saying this.

"You have given us so much and no matter what you choose, we love you."

What I really want to say is, *"Dad, I'm sorry I've been so busy lately with my new job. I'm sorry I haven't called home in a while. I'm sorry for losing hope last night during my moment alone. I pray my lack of faith didn't lead to this. I hope you don't think I took you for granted. I will regret not calling you more often for the rest of my life."*

I can go on for a life-time with my guilt, but I can't say any of it out loud, not in front of Kristen or these nurses. I feel shitty enough about myself; I don't need anyone else judging me.

Kristen

Speaking to my dad only makes my guilt worse.

I should be telling him, *"I'm sorry for not coming home last weekend, Dad. Or the weekend before. I shouldn't have gone to the St. Patty's Day bar crawl. I should've been at home watching a murder mystery show with you, eating your famous popcorn, guessing who the killer is."*

The lump in my throat grows bigger.

"I will regret coming home one weekend too late for the rest of my life."

Why can't I say this out loud? Why am I avoiding the truth?

I guess I don't want Thomas to know how badly I fucked up.

| 11:21 PM |

Natalie

When Thomas and Kristen come back, they seem even more distraught than before. Both of them are crying so hard I can barely hear them breathing anymore. *Did they say their goodbyes? Did the priest convince them to go say goodbye?*

"Mom, can I please talk to you outside. Now." I hope she can hear the urgency in my voice. We need to fix this before Dad thinks they are okay with any other decision than him making it out of here alive.

She meets me outside, but she won't look up at me.

"Mom, we can't listen to him. He's a stranger. He doesn't know our family. I know Dad can make it out of here."

"No one is giving up, Natalie."

Brandon comes out of the private waiting room.

"Mrs. Owen, would it be okay if I went to see Mr. Owen?"

I forgot he hasn't seen him since we'd gotten here.

"Of course, honey. Do you want someone to come with you?"

"No, this is something I would prefer to do alone."

Is Mom forgetting about our conversation? I look at her closely, trying to figure out where she is mentally. *She has to agree with me. We have to be on the same page before it's too late.*

Once Brandon starts to walk away, she returns her attention back to me to finish our conversation.

"Let's say a prayer together."

She takes my hand and gives it a squeeze. The coldness of her hand sends shivers down my spine. *Why is it freezing in here?*

"I think we both need it right now."

> *I don't really have time for this. We need to talk to Dad; tell him we absolutely need him. But I don't want to fight my mom too much. I also need her. I need her on my side.*

"Dear Father, we don't understand your plan. We trust you and we don't ask for you to explain your purpose."

> *Well no, I do want to know the purpose of this.*

"We ask for your guidance. We ask for you to shed light on our fears and help bring us together during this time. We pray for strength and courage when we feel small and anxious. We pray that we turn to you instead of away from you…"

I stop listening as her last few words sink in.

"We pray that we turn to you instead of away from you."

> *Am I turning away from God? Am I interjecting in His plan?*

No.

No.

No.

I am helping him, I am helping my family, I am helping me.

Tuning her out, I start my own prayer in my head. *"God, please. I promise to never question your plans ever again. Just please."*

A tear sneaks up and falls out of the corner of my right eye.

"Please."

With my eyes raised, I ask one more time.

"Please don't take my dad, not yet."

119

- EIGHT -

Brandon

The priest's words keep replaying in my mind, "Don't leave anything left unsaid." It's all I can hear sitting in the waiting room. It's painted on the walls, it's buzzing from the clock, it's everywhere.

It feels like he was speaking directly at me when he said it. My mind races back to February; the last time Natalie and I were in Charlotte.

I was invited to a job fair by the southern private schools in the Charlotte area. Natalie was over the moon for me; probably because she was just as much involved in the job application process as I had been. She helped me create my resumé and cover letter a month prior. She went as far as creating a LinkedIn profile for me. She always pushed for my success as hard as she did for her own. Her motivation is one of the main reasons I love her as much as I do. *She never gives up on anything.*

When she found out about the fair, she said we had to go, no matter what. So, we did. We left on a Thursday afternoon and drove the entire way to her parents'. It'd been about a month since she last came home, and being far away from home was slowly killing Natalie. Plus, we were about to tell her parents about our plans to go to Punta Cana in March. We both knew they would be upset to hear that she wasn't coming home for spring break, and truthfully, I think she was having her own second thoughts about the trip, too. But either way, the airline tickets were purchased, so hopefully, this weekend trip would soften the blow. On Friday night, I had a happy hour with the recruiters. By the time I came home, my face hurt from smiling for hours and my small talk was worn out. All I wanted to do was eat dinner and go straight to bed.

As soon as I walked inside from the garage, I knew my ideal plan wasn't going to happen. I heard the entire Owen family howling at the dinner table. They were laughing a bit too hard and the music was a tad too loud. Before making it fully to the kitchen, I realized it was their usual family game night. I wasn't in the mood to play cards, but I grabbed some leftovers from the fridge and sat down at the table anyway.

"How was the networking hour?" Natalie asked. Her words asked genuinely, but I didn't feel like going into the details in front of everyone. Thanks to baseball, ever since I was little, I've been superstitious. The last thing I wanted to do was jinx myself on any possible opportunities.

So, my response was short and to the point. "It was fine. I think I'll find out more tomorrow." I was exhausted and I thought it was obvious in my voice.

Kristen spoke next. "I'm so excited y'all are moving down here!" She adores Natalie, even though Natalie never thinks so, and I knew she was happy to have her close again. They all were. Mr. Owen always talked about this upcoming summer with such excitement. All of the kids would be back in the same city again. He already planned three vacations to celebrate.

Natalie received a job offer six months before starting her master's program. She had committed to Charlotte before we ever talked about how serious we were. But I'd follow her anywhere and she knew it.

I smiled back at Kristen. I was too drained to answer her.

A hard smack on the table made me sit up straight and widen my eyes. It threw me off and I almost spilled the beef stew shaking in my spoon. I was awake now. Searching for the noise, my eyes fell on Mr. Owen's hand on the table. I remember how red it was from the hit.

"Listen here, Brandon. This is the real deal. No more messing around."

Where was he going with this? I looked at Natalie but she wouldn't meet my eyes. No one would. *What's going on?*

"You can't be going into this half-hearted."

I could feel my heart rate rising. *Obviously I knew that, Mr. Owen. It wasn't like I didn't want to get a job.*

Mrs. Owen stepped in, "Corey, he knows it's serious. This isn't your place."

I remember Natalie telling me her dad could be hard on them sometimes. She told me how upset she got in sixth grade when he yelled at her for saying she wanted to move to California and work on a beach when she grew up. When she told me the story, I couldn't help but laugh. *How could she not realize her dad only wanted the best for her?* He wanted her to be independent, not needing someone in her life to support her. *Why would she get so upset about her dad simply caring?* The memory of his disappointment stuck with Natalie forever. She completely changed her aspirations that day and never looked back.

"I'm serious," Mr. Owen continued. "It's the bottom of the ninth and there's two outs. You need to step up to the plate."

Okay, I get it. I was getting the infamous "California talk." I needed a job--I knew that--but all of this pressure wasn't going to help me sleep any better before the job fair tomorrow.

The awkwardness in the room was apparent. I was annoyed that Natalie didn't stand up for me. She knew how hard we had prepped for this fair. As everyone started to head to bed, Mr. Owen called me into the office.

"Brandon, I'm serious. You better take care of my little girl."

Did he not think I was enough?

I never let go of my anger from that night. I was mad that he had made me feel like I wasn't good enough for Natalie. Yet now, as we sit here, it all makes sense. *How couldn't I see it before?* I need to go talk to him; tell him I'm sorry for holding this grudge for so long.

Racing out of the room, I can barely keep my thoughts in line. Nearly running into Natalie, I ask Mrs. Owen if I can go speak to him. I don't want to interrupt any family time, but I need to stress the urgency. I need to talk

123

to him. Now.

When I turn the corner, I stop to take a breath, calm my nerves before entering his room. I'm not sure if I'm ready to see him so sick and fragile, but apologizing is all I can think about. It's pushing me forward. *The nurses are probably going to wonder who I am since I don't resemble the Owen family at all.* I enter the room slowly. Not one head turns to face me. Not one set of eyes rise to greet me at the door. The nurses don't notice I've entered the space to talk to Mr. Owen; they're all consumed with their own tasks. *I was hoping it could be a bit more private, but I'll take what I can get.*

I am at a loss for words when I finally reach his bedside. *This doesn't even slightly resemble the man I've known for the last five years.* His face looks completely different; it's swollen and ghostly pale. The swelling around his eyes makes it appear as if it would be impossible for him to open his eyes, no matter how much he tried. *I think I might pass out.* I feel guilty for seeing him this vulnerable. My head sinks and I have to look down; I can't bear to stare at his face any longer. His hands don't provide much more comfort. The swelling of his fingers make his wedding band look like it is cutting off blood circulation. *He's too weak to do anything about it.* I turn to the wall; I'm not sure where to direct my eyes anymore.

My tears feel cold on my face. *Stop crying, you have to be strong.*

"Mr. Owen, I hope you're not mad I came to see you."

> *He's probably pissed people are seeing him this way, especially his kids.*

"On the brighter side, I decided to switch out of my Eagles shirt from this morning."

Kristen had been the first one to notice my shirt this morning. She said it might be a good thing I was wearing it; the sight of it would piss him off enough to wake him up from the sedation. But, now, I'm not sure anything can wake him up from the induced coma-- not even Natalie taking his Audi for a spin.

"I just wanted to come in and tell you..." I stop.

Why can't I keep going? My throat is closing in and I wonder if I have enough room to breathe anymore. *Come on Brandon, get it together.* I remind myself of the priest's words. *Don't leave anything left unsaid.*

"I want you to know how sorry I am for being upset with you for this long. It's your job as a dad to be protective over your girls. I know I'm not good enough for Natalie,"

I pause to gather my composure before carrying on.

"But I will do everything in my power to give her what she deserves. I will care for her even when she's being stubborn, I will be there to listen to her vent when she gets pissed off, and I will be enough of a man to step back and watch her career succeed beyond mine."

Mr. Owen always talks about how successful he thought she could be. I know he wants to make sure I would be okay with her being the breadwinner. But, more importantly, I know he wants to make sure I understand my broader responsibility... her family.

"I'll be there when Kristen brings home a guy. I will question his intentions as much as you did with me."

I have to take a break to wipe my nose with my sleeve. *Fuck, this is harder than I imagined.*

"I'll be there for Thomas when he needs a wingman. I'll even pick up the wings for Sunday football."

This is quite a commitment, Mr. Owen.

"Unless the Eagles are playing."

Damn it, I know that won't be enough for him.

"Fine, I'll make an exception but it's going to have to be the wing place down the road even if they aren't as good as the wings off Providence Road."

The slightest chuckle spits out of my throat, and I can feel the

125

tension in the room lighten.

"I'll take care of the yard for Mrs. Owen, and step up to support your girls when Thomas has to travel."

"I will prove myself to you for the rest of my life."

I need to thank him for everything he has given me in case I never have the chance to again.

"Thank you for letting me come on countless family vacations. Thanks for making me feel welcomed from the first day I drove down to meet everyone, thanks for pushing me to be a better man for Natalie, and thanks for always giving me shit for being an Eagles fan."

Thanks for being a role model of a loving husband, of a supportive father.

"I love Natalie, Mr. Owen. I love your family. I'll do my best to take care of them."

No one will do as good of a job as you have. No one will be able to provide the lifestyle you have. Fuck.

I wipe my eyes before leaving the room, but I know it doesn't help. I can't stop the tears from pouring down my face. I try to sniff any evidence of my runny nose, but it'll be impossible to hide it. *I have to get a job before I graduate. Everything is on the line now.*

| 11:34 PM |

Natalie

My prayer is interrupted as my mom starts walking away. *Did she finish her prayer?*

Jolting my head around, I watch her wrap her arms around Brandon. Tension softens in my body as I realize how much pain everyone is in. I can't remember if I've ever seen Brandon cry this hard.

Why is he crying so hard?

What is going on?

My mind starts sprinting to possible answers. *Is Dad still alive?*

Sprinting towards his room, my heart drops when I can finally make out the familiar beeping of his monitors.

Thank goodness. My breathing is loud and heavy. *I thought he might be gone.* Hunched over, I try to slow down my heart rate. *Why is Brandon crying so hard then?*

I take my time making my way over to him. Another one of the walls I strategically built around my heart falls down with each step. Along with it come all of the tears I have been trying so desperately to hold in. The tears slowly leave the corner of my eyes and trickle down the side of my face onto my neck. I don't try to stop it from falling; I don't wipe away the wet remains from my face. The feeling it leaves behind reminds me I'm not dreaming. I need to stay focused on telling my dad to keep holding on.

"Dad, it's me."

Staring at his unfamiliar features, I vigorously shake my head trying to remain focused.

"Listen, I know you're going to make it out of here okay."

There is no other option. He has to survive this bleed.

"This surgery is going to stop the bleeding. I need you to be strong. I need you to fight through this. I need you to…"

I know I'm being selfish; I'm telling him what I need without thinking about what he needs.

But I can't help myself.

"I need you, Dad. We all do."

127

My eyes squeeze tightly shut, and I begin making a deal.

If he just fights through this, if he just makes it out of this, I promise I'll never ask him to fight again. I'll never ask You again. But he can't stop fighting now. I can't say goodbye to him like this. I need to hear him say goodbye back to me; squeeze my hand and tell me I need to stop stressing myself out. I need him to tell me the secrets to navigate my way to a successful career; tell me what exactly is in his hot salsa or secret popcorn sauce. There is so much I still need to learn from him. I need to hear him sing Folsom Blues one more time and call me about some lyrics he crafted at three in the morning. I need to hear him tell me he loves me one last time. I can't walk away from my dad like his. I'm not giving up hope, because I know this isn't how it is supposed to end; it can't be.

I feel a tap on my shoulder, "Ma'am, we are going to need you to leave soon. We need to do the last steps for sterilization."

The nurse's eyes widen when I turn around. I'm sure mascara's rubbed all over my face. Nodding my head, I lean down, making sure he can hear me.

"Dad, I will see you after surgery. Please, Dad. *No one* has given up on you, *no one.*"

I choke on the last words, "I love you."

My mind is full of regrets as I walk out of the room. *You should've said sorry. Told him how sorry you are for not coming home over spring break. Punta Cana wasn't even worth it. I should've said I'm sorry for going to school in Erie; I should've stayed near home.* "I'll tell him I'm sorry when he wakes up tomorrow," I reassure myself under my breath. I need him to hear me say it, not these nurses that don't know my name. Plus, I'm already judging myself for failing as a daughter; I don't need strangers to judge me, too.

As soon as I walk out of his room, I notice two staff members hanging yellow caution tape at the end of the hallway. *What the hell is going on?* I squint to read the sign, "Surgery in Process. Hall is Closed."

My knees buckle and I hit the floor. My emotions spill out once more, and there's no stopping them now. I rest my head in between my knees and I begin to hyperventilate with every sob. *I don't even know what to feel anymore; what to do anymore.* I'm tired and confused. Right now, I feel completely vulnerable. The footsteps of a stranger walk past me and stop. When my eyes meet his, I can tell he pities me. *I wonder if I look as shitty as the girl I had seen a few hours ago.*

Just wait, you will have your time on the floor crying like an idiot soon enough, I think to myself. *There's no way of masking your emotions in this place.*

TOP DOWN DAY

Part III

SUNDAY

MARCH 24TH

- NINE -

Thomas

The room's heavy with pain and no one is saying much, except for the priest, of course. He keeps awkwardly trying to make dialogue with everyone. Thank goodness my grandparents are here to engage in conversation because no one else has the energy to entertain him.

The best part is when Father asks for all our names and some back-story on how old we are, if we're in school or working, and whatever other question he thinks is pertinent to understanding who we are. If that isn't awkward enough, he follows it with "Learning more about us helps give better guidance." *Can he really not tell how awkward he is making us feel? We can't openly talk about what we're thinking because of him.* With every additional question, it becomes clearer how much of a stranger he really is. It feels odd to have someone sit with us that can barely even remember our last name during one of our most vulnerable moments. Natalie walks into our room. *Thank God for the interruption; it was almost my turn to give him my five-minute life story.* Everyone redirects their attention to her swollen eyes and slouched back.

"We can't go into the room anymore…"

She takes a moment to regroup, letting out a sigh.

"Something about sterilizing."

Her eyes carry an immense amount of pain. Each one red and outlined with tired wrinkles. Her neck looks blotchy. I wonder if her throat feels as tight as mine does.

"Thank you, Father, for your time. You have helped us tremendously."

I shoot a look at my mom. *She has to be joking right?*

133

She continues, "I think we need some time to ourselves right now. But, thank you again."

Father responds, "Of course. I'm just glad the hospital called me."

So, that's who called him. I figured my mom or grandma had called for a priest.

"I will keep you in my prayers."

Hopefully he can keep our names straight.

"God Bless."

Mom follows him out of the room, closing the door gently behind her.

I hear Kristen laugh nervously as the door latches, "That was painfully weird."

Laughter swarms the room as everyone acknowledges the tension. *I wonder what people passing by think when they hear the private room busting out laughing.*

Dawn

"Thank you again for coming." *I know he hasn't been the most helpful, but it gives me peace to have a priest with us tonight.*

"Of course. I wish you the best and, like I said, I'll keep you and your family in my prayers."

"Father, there is one last thing."

I can't help my fingers from fidgeting with my wedding ring.

"I know I explained earlier how Corey isn't Catholic, but I was wondering if you had time to give him his last rites if by any chance he passes away."

I'd rather be safe than sorry.

"Unfortunately, I can't. I won't even be able to give him a final blessing because he isn't practicing. I can stand outside of his room and pray for his soul with you, but I can't go into his room and read him his last rites."

My heart stops before it drops. My entire body tightens as I process what this priest has just said to me. *You have got to be kidding me!*

I wonder if Father can see the rage building up inside of me. He better leave this hospital soon because my tongue is about to start bleeding as I bite down on it, holding back how I really feel. *My husband is not someone who will contaminate you. He is a loving father who gives his all to everyone around him. How dare you tell me you can't go into his room and pray with him his rites! It's priests like you that cause the number of practicing Catholics to decline. It's not up to you to decide who makes it into heaven; you don't get to pick who can receive their last rites. If the entrance to heaven is based solely on how good of a practicing Catholic you are and not about the purity of your soul, then God help **all** of us.*

"You know what…"

My eyes narrow as the glare sets in.

"That won't be necessary."

How sad that in my time of greatest need a man of the collar is turning his back on me.

| 1:17 AM |

Thomas

At this point, my legs have probably run three marathons with how vigorously I am shaking them. I have counted every tile on the floor and ceiling as I try to avoid eye contact with everyone else, trying to process what is going on around me.

My mom keeps rambling, "We all need to go to bed. It's still going to be awhile until the surgery starts and the doctor warned me it's going to be a long procedure."

135

Her head turns around the room, searching for agreement.

"It's already Sunday," she continues.

I can't believe it's already Sunday.

Grandma looks up at her, "We can come back in the morning and go to 8 AM mass at the church down the street."

Going to church is the last thing I feel like doing. Especially if it means there is a possibility of running into Father. I don't think I can ever look at him without thinking about his snow globe monologue. I still don't get how we're supposed to find comfort in comparing our lives to snowflakes, but maybe I wasn't paying enough attention to grasp the ultimate meaning of the parable. *I'll give him the benefit of the doubt.*

My grandpa stands up with my grandma and tells Mom, "Call us if anything changes." They both make their rounds among us, passing out hugs and kisses.

Once they leave the room, Kristen breaks the silence. "I'm not going anywhere. I can sleep on the couch."

"Where will Mom sleep then?" I respond back to her. I know the surgeon isn't going to let her into Dad's room, at least not until the surgery is over.

Without hesitation, she answers. "I'll take the chair, the floor, I don't care." Her voice has tiredness and anger interwoven.

"Listen, everyone is going home. I will call you when the surgery is over and you can come back to see him. I need everyone well-rested." Mom sounds more serious now.

She keeps saying that she needs everyone well rested, but I'm starting to wonder if she needs time alone. Time to process. Time to think.

Natalie looks exhausted, but equally serious. "You have to call us if anything changes and after every single update, big or small. Even if it's just a nurse telling you how much longer until the procedure is over."

I watch as her eyes soften before meeting Mom's eyes.

"Please."

"I know, I will." Mom's voice is as fragile as her body appears.

I know she doesn't intentionally leave us in the dark.

"Seriously, go. I can't fall asleep if everyone stays."

Mom knows when she says that, it will convince us all to leave. We're all concerned with the little amount of sleep she is getting, and we'll do anything to help her get even a minute of rest.

Brandon hugs my mom and she kisses him on the check. *I hope Brandon knows how grateful we are to have him here.* No one else has the energy to console Kristen or put up with Natalie's mood swings. If he wasn't here to step up and be there for everyone when they are falling apart, I can't imagine how this would be going right now. I can't imagine how many f-bombs my grandparents would have to listen to before they each had a heart attack.

Kristen

The elevator ride seems incredibly slow in the parking garage. It has just enough shakiness to make you wonder if this is going to be the trip it decides to break.

"My gut is telling me Dad is going to be okay." Natalie doesn't look up from the floor when she begins to speak.

When no one answers, she raises her head up. Her eyes are wide and she looks scared. Her voice sounded so confident; *yet her facial expression is telling a different story.*

"I'm serious guys. I have such a good feeling."

She isn't looking for someone to agree with her; she's looking for someone to reassure her. I don't have the strength to be that person for her.

137

"That's great Natalie. I think it's important to trust your gut." Thomas is trying to protect her. *We can't let her be so naïve.*

I begin to answer, "I'm honestly not sure anymore." But when my eyes lock with Natalie's eyes I change my mind. *Maybe she isn't naïve, maybe she is right. Maybe I am being too quick to give up.* "But… I do know Dad can do anything he sets his mind to."

Is this really Dad's decision?

Brandon chimes in, "I think it's great the doctors haven't given up hope and they keep wanting to perform more surgeries. I think that's a really good sign."

The prior ICU doctor's words flash through my mind. *"Tonight is a different story."*

If only he heard what the ICU doctor told me before the transfer. Are we the ones that keep deciding to stay on this roller coaster ride of emotions? We convince ourselves we hear good news when really we haven't?

Natalie begins to smile and eagerly shakes her head in agreement, "Yeah, me too." She takes Brandon's hand, pulls him close, and whispers, "I think it's all going to be alright."

I redirect to the floor. I can't watch her anymore.

Damn, I hope she is right.

| 1:48 AM |

Kristen

By the time we make it home to Mom's house, Natalie and Brandon are already asleep in the back seat. With a gentle nudge, Thomas wakes them up, and we all head to separate rooms. My bedroom feels so cold and lonely. *Natalie is lucky she has Brandon with her.* She never dated anyone before him, and we all joked in high school that her first boyfriend would be the man she marries.

I wish I had someone beside me right now, someone to make me feel less isolated. I reach for my phone and find Matt's number. We dated my freshman and sophomore year of college. Natalie wasn't a fan of him from the start, but she is always so critical of my boyfriends. I ignore the idea of her distaste, and draft a message anyways.

I want to talk to him right now. *I need someone to comfort me. I need someone who knows my dad and the constant rollercoaster his hospital visits bring me.* I text him, "you up by any chance?" but before I hear my phone ding with his response, my body succumbs to my exhaustion, and I fall asleep.

|2:29 AM|

Dawn

My eyes slowly start to open. The room is so bright. I need a minute to adjust my eyes to the lighting. I look down at my watch to see what time it is, but it's charging in the back corner when it died a few hours ago. I can't remember where I put my phone. *How long have I been asleep? Did the surgery begin?* Wrapping my head around each question, adrenaline rushes through my body and hoists me off the couch.

I sprint into the hallway, looking for someone to give me an update. A flash of blackness falls like a blanket over my vision, and I realize I must've gotten up too quickly from a deep sleep. When my blurred vision returns, I notice the yellow caution tape is still hanging and chairs are blocking anyone from going beyond the roped-off hallway. The only people I can see are nurses outside of the room waiting to help if needed.

There is a crowd of additional nurses and doctors in Corey's room. No one even notices I'm making my way down the hallway because the room's commotion is consuming all of their attention. I can peek through the Venetian blinds when I jump high enough. I find immense comfort in being able to see Corey again. *I'm right here, Corey; I'm watching from right here.*

139

I hear a voice call out, "It's all black, doctor. What should we do?"

Another voice firmly responds, "Remove it."

Remove what? I start jumping higher and faster now. My breath gets heavier with each leap.

"Mrs. Owen?" One nurse spots me in the hall; her eyes squinting trying to make sure it's really me. I recognize her. She's the one who pulled me into the private room last night. She told me the doctor needed to open the wound again to see what he's dealing with before assessing the next steps.

The doctor orders an assistant to do something, but I can't make out his voice anymore. I watch the assistant slowly approach the window. Suddenly, my brain pieces it together; he is drawing the blinds so they can't see me jumping up and down like a lunatic. The man looks at me with the coldest eyes I've ever seen. He doesn't even break eye contact as he pulls the blinds shut. I can't tell if he is disgusted with me or pities me.

The sight of Corey is officially gone; the only bit of comfort I had is now completely taken away from me. *I can't see Corey! I can't protect him!*

"No! Don't close the blinds! You can't do this!"

    This is my fucking right!

"Someone needs to tell me what is going on right now! I am his wife! I have rights! My husband has rights! I need to protect him!"

    None of the nurses sitting outside the room will face me; none dare to look me in the eyes. They don't realize I'm not going to stop making a scene until someone tells me what is going on and why I'm being left in the dark... alone and confused.

"Look at me!" I scream. "Tell me what the hell is going on... *right now!*"

My grief is being pushed to the side by my newfound anger. *Why the hell didn't someone come wake me up? I should've been told when the surgery was beginning! What are they hiding from me?!*

As my head is spinning, I notice a nurse turn her head towards me. Her blonde hair tightly pulled back in a ponytail. Her tired eyes meet mine. Sympathy is radiating from her green eyes, and in this moment I can feel her trying so desperately to take away some of my sorrow. "I'm so sorry ma'am. I will get one of the doctors in the room to come out immediately and give you an update."

I think she can tell I'm contemplating jumping over the chairs.

"Please, just wait in the hallway. You can't come beyond the tape for safety matters."

I blurt out, "How long has he been in surgery?"

I don't wait for a response before continuing.

"Why didn't someone wake me up?"

"Ma'am, I'll go get a doctor to come talk to you."

I'm not accepting that answer, not anymore. I'm tired of being left in the dark trying to figure this out on my own. I demand again, "How long has he been in surgery?!"

The discontent is written all over my face, but yet, she pauses before answering. *How hard of a question is this to answer?*

"Sit right here. I will be right back."

I watch her race into the room. *At least she's trying.* When she exits the room, a doctor accompanies her. I cross my arms; *this doctor better have some answers. No more backing down.*

She begins to introduce herself, "Hello, Mrs. Owen, I'm Dr. Findley."

Her white teeth shine as she greets me with a smile. Her long dark hair nearly completely hidden under her scrub cap.

"I have been pulled to assist in your husband's case."

I don't care what your name is or where you did your rotations. I care about my husband, and why the hell no one came to wake me up when the surgery began.

"How long has he been in surgery?"

Third time's the charm.

"He has been in surgery for about twenty minutes."

She calmly checks her watch to confirm her estimation.

"We were planning on getting you when we had an update.

I wish I believed you, but I don't.

We weren't sure what we were dealing with, and truthfully, we needed time to assess the situation."

Her mouth still upward and her eyes light, not showing any glimpse of remorse.

"I would've liked to have been woken up when the surgery began. I would've liked to have been awake when my husband gets cut open once again."

Her eyes fall and her mouth clinches finally showing a sign of regret. "I completely understand, Mrs. Owen." She begins nodding her head and adding, "I apologize and it won't happen again." Her response finally seems to be genuine.

"Well, what is going on? What does the main doctor think?"

I can't remember his name, and I'm embarrassed I have to resort to calling him the 'main doctor.'

"Unfortunately, the bleeding is worse than we expected."

Her pause feels intentional. She's letting the information settle in before continuing.

"The prolonged bleeding has caused the kidneys and liver to fail. Dialysis treatment will continue as soon as we finish."

The news breaks whatever is left of my heart. Lifetime dialysis treatment was the reason Corey and his family let his mother pass away.

They knew it wasn't a life his mom would have wanted to live. The constant treatments put such a strain on her mental health. *Did we ever talk about if he would mind being on dialysis? If he could handle the frequent follow ups and restrictions?*

She goes on, "It is apparent his stomach has also suffered greatly from the bleed. When we unpacked his wound, the stomach was already turning black. It was too late to save the organ, so we had to remove it."

The room starts to spin, their faces aren't staying still, and I can't hear her voice over the ringing. *They removed his stomach! I knew this was a possibility but shouldn't they have consulted me before going ahead with it?*

I can hear her saying something about the intestines turning gray and removing some of the length in both the small and large intestine. She talks about the next step in the surgery-- Abdominoperineal Resection.

Is it legal to make these decisions without consulting his wife?!

When she starts talking about his brain activity, I can't listen to it anymore. "Stop it! What the hell are you thinking!"

Her eyes widen and she takes a step back. I can only imagine what she's thinking of me right now, but I don't give a damn. She looks just as confused as she does shocked. *Welcome to the club, I am just as confused, doctor.*

I continue to scream, "Don't you think you should have woken me up before deciding which of his organs you should keep and which should be removed?!"

She isn't answering; my fist clenches harder as I wait for her reaction. All of the anger I have been holding in is coming out.

"What about his quality of life?! Would you want to live without a stomach, without intestines, without a colon?"

My hands are making sweeping movements as I describe each organ, emphasizing the importance of these decisions they've been making without my consent.

She still looks stunned; her mouth has slightly opened now but she still

143

doesn't utter a word. *I can keep going all night.*

"Why did I have to bring his living will if no one is going to even look at it! He signed that he didn't want extraordinary measures taken! He doesn't want any heroic acts or to be forced to live on this Earth because some doctor, who let me remind you, doesn't even know him or his love for wings which he obviously can't eat anymore without a God damn stomach, decides *they* know best!"

I'm crying now and spit is flying out of my mouth with every sentence. Every word is physically hurting my body. My throat is raspy from yelling and my chest feels like it might explode. *Can you actually die from heartbreak?*

"I'm so sorry Mrs. Owen."

She takes a breath before continuing,

"You're right. You are absolutely right."

I watch her shake her head with every word.

"I'm going to get Dr. Thompson."

That's his name. Now I remember it.

"Take the time to think about what is best for you and your family."

What about what is best for Corey? Shouldn't his opinion matter too?

Dr. Findley begins to head back to the room, but she turns around one last time and says, "I really am sorry. Sometimes we get so wrapped up in the trauma and doing anything and everything to save the life of the person lying on the table that sometimes we forget about their life once the surgery is over." She almost looks disappointed in herself.

I know that look too well.

Dawn

I'm alone now; only me and my thoughts. In the dark hallway, I'm trying to take Dr. Findley's advice and think about what is best for Corey and us.

Living without a stomach doesn't seem like a life Corey would want to be a part of. He would have to retire, and his daily living tasks would consume both of our lives. *Would he ever wake up from this coma? If he does, would he be the same person? If Corey is ready to see his mom and sister, I don't want to be the driving force keeping him in this world--and away from them--any longer.*

But if we let him pass peacefully, what would happen to us? Would I need to get a job after twenty-one years of being a stay-at-home mom? Would I need to sell the house where we've been creating family memories?

I can go back and get a job. I can find a realtor. That doesn't scare me. What really scares me is if Corey will hate me if I make the wrong decision.

I can't form tears anymore. I feel so anxious about this decision, and I can't stop agonizing over which option has the least shitty outcome. *I can't make this decision alone; I need help from someone who knows us, really knows us.*

I hear the other line ruffle before Savannah picks up the call, "Dawn? Are you there?"

Her voice calms my stomach immediately. Savannah is the type of friend who you don't need to talk to every day but when you finally have the chance to sit down and catch up, it doesn't feel like a day has ever passed by. I hated almost everything about Pennsylvania when we moved. The weather was always grey, the temperature stayed cold for too long. On the day we found out we were moving to Charlotte, I was over-the-moon excited. I was ready to live in a warmer climate and wake up to the Carolina blue skies every morning. I called to tell Savannah the good news before anyone else. After the first ring, I realized what this move meant. It meant I was moving away from my neighbor of eighteen years, the woman who I raised my children alongside. The neighbor who co-planned every holiday party we ever hosted. Savannah was there for me when I lost my grandmother and I was there for her when she had a stillbirth. We were bonded together through the terrible, terrible middle school days with our daughters. I sobbed when I told her I was leaving, but she promised we would stay in touch, and so we have.

"Yeah, I'm here. I'm so sorry for waking you."

"Is everything okay?" I can tell she's woken up from a deep sleep. She sounds disoriented.

I keep forgetting that no one outside of family knows the hell we have been living in the past few days. *It's so nice to hear a fresh voice.* I need Savannah to be a voice of reason; a voice removed from the family who hasn't been tainted by the weekend's rollercoaster of emotions.

"No, Savannah."

I begin to let go.

"Nothing is okay anymore."

Nothing is ever going to be okay.

She listens to me cry before probing me with questions. "What happened, Dawn?" Her voice sounds so calm.

"Corey is in the hospital."

My voice sounds exhausted.

"He's been bleeding... "

The sobs take voice and I have to take a break before continuing.

"...internally since Friday."

It sounds surreal when I finally say it out loud. My husband has been bleeding from his gastric artery, a main artery outlining his stomach, for three straight days. *How the hell is this happening?*

146

"Oh my God, Dawn!"

She doesn't sound calm anymore.

"I can't believe it."

Savannah is crying into the phone now.

"I just can't believe it."

Does she already have an idea of how bad it's gotten? I guess a call at nearly four in the morning isn't necessarily a good sign.

"The doctors have removed his spleen, stomach, and part of his large and small intestines."

My words fly out of my mouth as fast as possible. I want to give her all of the details but I want to get it over with quickly. *Speaking about his organs make me want to vomit.*

"His kidney and liver are failing. He will have to be on dialysis for the rest of his life. *The rest of his life.* And his brain activity doesn't look good."

I have to stop and take a breath. I've been focusing on telling her everything, I've forgotten to breathe.

"It doesn't look good, Savannah."

I let out a whimper before I continue.

"On Saturday, he scored a 4 on a neurological scale that, I guess, reads the state of a person's consciousness. Now he's at a 3, meaning he's completely unresponsive, Savannah, *completely unresponsive.*"

There is a ruffle over the phone and I swear I can hear her heartbeat. *Did she drop the phone to her chest?*

"Oh, Dawn." I listen as she whimpers out.

My heart is aching as I think back on it all. "Corey has been sedated since Friday and as of right now, he has received just over 40 units of blood."

147

Savannah doesn't answer as she tries to digest everything I have thrown at her.

"Oh, and I just freaked out on the doctors trying to save his life. So, I'm really succeeding as a wife right now."

"Dawn, don't say that! You are a great wife and Corey knows that."

Does he though?

"So, what is next?"

That's a great question. That's why I called you.

"I'm not sure. The doctors are giving me time to think about what's the best decision for our family. I'm torn between the options; neither seem like the right answer."

What I really should be asking is if she can make the decision for me, because either way I don't think I'll be able to live with myself and the what-ifs that are sure to follow.

"Oh, Dawn. I can't believe you have to make this decision right now. I really don't know what to say."

"Savannah, you know Corey better than most people. I need you to tell me if you think he would want to live without his stomach. It would be a life with a feeding tube and a colostomy bag if the surgery continues."

I try to imagine it, but I can't.

"It would be a lifetime of battling infections without his spleen to fight off any bacteria. He may never breathe on his own again."

I know my answer before she responds.

"No, Dawn. There is no way Corey, or anyone for that sake, would want to live a life like that."

I take a long, deep breath before responding. I know she is right, but it feels so raw to finally hear someone else say it out loud. *Corey wouldn't want this. We have to do what is best for him. We have to let go.*

148

"Okay, I'm going to go make the hardest decision of my life."

The phone call ends.

- TEN -

Dawn

The hallway seems to get darker. Lonelier. The cold walls are supporting me from falling. My phone screen blinding my eyes as they try to adjust to the lighting. *Why isn't there dim lighting in here?*

Every muscle in my body is holding me back from dialing the next few phone numbers, but I need to do this for Corey. *It's my obligation as his wife to try to stop his suffering-- right?* But I know I have a list of people who need to confirm that this is the right decision; we need to be on the same page. It's the only way any of us will be able to wake up the next morning, and the morning after that.

The first phone call is going to be the hardest of them all.

I'm glad they decided to leave last night. Corey wouldn't want them to be here when it's time to make the decision. They would never be able to let go if they were still here, especially if they started to think about what exactly they would be losing. *Am I even thinking about what we would be losing? Thomas will lose the one who taught him to love every sport out there, the one who encouraged him to learn to play the guitar. Natalie will lose her life coach, the one who understands her wittiness and pushes her grit. Kristen will lose her binge-watching best friend, the one who plays the guitar while she sings to the rest of us. How will I ever fill his role for each of my kids? I can't play the guitar, I don't have his humor, and I hate murder mystery series.*

And me? What will I be losing? *I will be losing my best friend, my confidant, my person, my everything.*

It feels like something is lodged in the back of my throat, but I'm too distracted by the loud ringing in my ears to pay much attention to it. My heart's beating out of my chest when I feel a vibration on my wrist. My

151

apple watch is notifying me of my high heart rate. *At least I'm in a hospital if my body decides to have a heart attack.*

Natalie

The ringing is loud; ear-piercing loud. I look around anxiously trying to pinpoint the source of the sound.

The hands aren't moving, not even the long one. This clock has to be broken. The talking in the room has gone silent. I can't even catch the shouting of his vitals anymore.

My sister isn't gasping for air in between each tear and I can't hear my brother trying to console her. *What is going on?*

I turn vigorously, searching for my Mom, searching for the sound, searching for answers.

Brandon is all I can see-- he is so close to my face, trying to comfort me, when really I just need him to get the fuck out of my way. *Where is my mom? Where is the sound? Where is the rewind button?* Everything goes black.

I wake up from my nightmare in a cold sweat with tears running down my face and fear shaking throughout my body. *Thank God it was just a dream.*

I must be crying pretty loudly because Brandon flips over and asks, "What's wrong?"

"Nothing. I'm sorry."

I have to take a breath in between each cry.

"Go back to bed."

"Another nightmare?"

I'm one of those anomalies who never grew out of the nightmare phase. Instead, mine have gotten worse; they have transformed from my dog dying to vivid dreams of being murdered or watching my sister get kidnapped. I'm well aware of how fucked up they are and it's why I don't tell many people about it. But when you're waking up paralyzed in fear with either drenched sheets or uncontrollable tears, it can be pretty hard to keep the secret from your boyfriend.

I whisper back, "Yeah." *Why am I so embarrassed?*

Brandon takes me into his arms and repeats, "It's okay, it was only a dream," over and over, like he normally does.

When I finally begin to catch my breath enough to calm down, my ears hear a distant ringing in another room. I almost confuse it for the ringing I've been hearing all weekend, until I hear Thomas answer, "Hello?"

Thomas

"Hello?"

I was sleeping so hard, I can barely distinguish if this is a dream or if I'm actually awake.

"Thomas, are the girls right there?"

I instantly recognize the voice, and I can feel the adrenaline flowing through my body as I shoot out of my bed.

"No; I'm getting them now."

I'm running to Kristen's room before I finish the sentence.

"Girls, get up!" I scream, "It's Mom."

I bang on Kristen's door and I hear her pop out of bed. Before I knock on Natalie's door, she and Brandon appear from behind it. *Had they never fallen asleep?*

We gather into the media room across from Kristen's bedroom, and I put the call on speakerphone. My thumbs are shaking so violently that I nearly end the call instead of hitting speaker.

"Okay, we're all together."

She isn't talking, just softly crying. We all look at each other; not knowing if we should ask her what's going on or wait for her to tell us when she's ready. The pit in my stomach is growing bigger as the silence drags on. *How much longer can this go on for?*

"Mom?" Kristen murmurs.

Mom blurts out, "I don't think he's going to make it, guys."

I don't know if I didn't hear her correctly or if my brain is fighting to convince myself it isn't real, but I'm about to ask her to repeat herself. Then I see my sisters. Kristen is gasping for air in between each tear. I want to console her, but I can't move. I feel stuck on the sofa, engulfed in the pain. I watch Brandon go to her and start rubbing her back. I turn my attention to Natalie. She looks paralyzed and cold, almost as if she's just seen a ghost. *She never wanted to give up hope, but now she is forced to.* I wondered if she heard Mom until I notice the tears silently running down her cheek. *She's heartbroken. They both are; we all are.*

Mom continues, "I need to know if you are okay with letting him go peacefully sooner rather than later. I'm not making any decisions until we all agree to what is best."

The silence in the room is deafening, so she asks again, "What do you think?"

Kristen answers first. "I think we should let him pass. He's suffered enough."

She takes a break to catch her breath and starts picking at her fingernails. Her nervous habits clearly portray her emotions despite her words saying to let him go.

She's whispering now, "Even if the doctors can ever stop the bleeding, which would be more than a miracle..."

She wipes the tears from her checks and rests her hands on her lap.

"...it's been too long."

Her tone sounds different now. It's analytical and precise. I can see her brain turning as she speaks from her clinical experience. *There is a noticeable disagreement between her brain and her heart. And I'm not sure which one I agree with.*

"His organs have gone days without proper blood flow."

The thought makes my stomach turn.

She is able to rationalize her thoughts because of her medical experience. She's thinking of Dad's quality of life because she's seen it ripped from so many others in the hospital. *I'm so impressed with her ability to separate her heart and her brain right now.*

"Thomas?" My mom asks.

I know what I need to say, but I don't feel ready. I wish she would just make the decision so we all didn't have to admit our acceptance out loud. *She knows we would respect whatever she decides to do, doesn't she?* Kristen is looking at me intently, waiting for my response.

"I agree with Kristen" is all I can manage to say before I choke on my words, and the tears I've been trying to hold in all spill out.

We can hear Mom take a deep breath before finally asking, "Natalie?"

Pausing before continuing.

"What do you think?"

Time seems to stop as we wait for her response. *We all know she's going to be the hardest one to get on board.* She's been clinging to hope this whole time, and I really think she convinced herself that he was going to make it out of this with no scrapes or bruises. I'm preparing what I'll rebut with if she says no. What words to strategically say to show her the *truth*.

Natalie answers so faintly, softer than a whisper; it's almost hard to hear, "Let him go."

Wow. Is that it?

My mom's voice comes through the phone one last time, "One more thing…"

What now? What more can we take?

"Are you all okay with what you said or do you need to come back for a final goodbye?"

Kristen

I can't even remember what I said last night, but I know I can't go back or I'm going to change my mind.

Natalie

I never even said goodbye. Should I tell him goodbye? Can I tell him goodbye? I don't want him to think I ever gave up hope.

Thomas

I don't think I can look at Dad knowing this will be the last time. I've already done that once this weekend and it nearly crushed me.

"Guys?" Mom is checking to see if we're still on the phone.

I look up at my sisters, who both look terrified by the thought of seeing him again. *That man in the hospital is not our dad, and it definitely isn't a memory we want to keep of him.*

"Sorry Mom," I answer back, "we are all shaking our heads over here. We're content with our last words."

That is what they wanted me to say, right?

Kristen

I hear Mom ending the call. "I'll call you with an update later. I love you all. So much. Goodbye."

No one is saying anything. We're all focusing on different parts of the walls surrounding us, not daring to look at each other. *What other updates would there be?*

Without much thought, I can hear my voice start to spill, "This doesn't feel real."

I don't want to bring everyone down with me, but I don't have any control over what I am saying.

Thomas speaks next. "I know. *What are we even going to do?*"

Before I can digest the question, Natalie responds. "I think we should pray."

Pray for what? His soul? God's plan? For us and the shitty days to follow?

Natalie starts us off, "Our Father, who art in Heaven..."

No one has the strength to say a prayer from our hearts. *How can I pray to something that is giving me so much pain right now?*

Yet, we all join in, "...Hallowed be thy name. Thy Kingdom come, thy will be done, on Earth as it is in Heaven."

Saying the familiar words, we sound in unity. *Sobbing through our words together. Asking for help together. Praying for Dad together.*

"Give us this day our daily bread and forgive us our trespasses…"

Their voices soften and eventually fade away. *Why did they stop? Did I mess something up? Give me strength to finish the prayer for us all.*

I'm the only one finishing the prayer, "...as we forgive those who trespass against us. Lead us not into temptation but deliver us from evil. Amen."

Are they tired? Confused? Giving up? No one utters another word, and I don't bother asking them what happened.

After nearly forty minutes of heavy silence, I scan the room.

We all lay in different spots on the three-piece sectional. It's quite the scene to see four mid-20 year olds all trying to fit onto one couch together. Everyone's feet are placed right above the next person's head. Brandon is holding Natalie tightly, too afraid to let her go. Suddenly, the ringing in my ears starts to get quieter. *The ring! I almost forgot to ask Natalie and Thomas if they've heard it!* I turn to ask Natalie and Thomas, but they are both passed out. Brandon with his arms still wrapped around Natalie, is also asleep. I grab my blanket and begin to close my eyes.

I don't have the energy to let my mind wander away. In a matter of minutes, we're all fast asleep. No more nightmares; no more ringing. Our heavy hearts are greeted with silence, and for once, peace.

| 4:04 AM |

Dawn

The hallway feels lighter, the coldness of the wall doesn't sting as much, when I hang up the phone. *The most dreadful conversation was over.* Yet, even with their approval, I still don't feel positive about the decision to stop the procedure. My knees are losing strength and the wall can't support all of me. I run my back along the wall and slowly meet my butt to the floor.

Should I let the doctors try one more time to stop the bleeding? Should I let the surgeons continue to remove organs to see if his body can survive without them? The next step would be removing his rectum because of the blood clots. My stomach turns as I think about this. *Kristen is right; his organs are damaged beyond repair. Corey could never be able to live a normal life again. Corey would resent me if I kept him in this world when he couldn't enjoy any ounce of what it has to offer. I would rather suffer the pain of losing him than put him through any second longer of physical pain. I need to move forward, so Corey can move forward.*

158

I search for Ed's number in my contacts.

Corey and his dad have always been close. I knew every Saturday morning Corey would be on the phone with his dad. Ed always treasures talking to Corey, especially after the losses they have suffered through together. Ed lost Corey's sister at seventeen to cancer. Losing a child is unimaginable, and I know Corey carried the pain of his sister's death every day of his life. Death has a funny way of always sticking around, reminding you of the ache when you think you have gotten one step ahead of it. Then, there was Corey's mother. She cherished her three children more than anything in the world. Two months before the girls were born, Corey's mom had gotten extremely sick. Her lupus had worsened and the doctors explained that the dialysis treatment was no longer going to be temporary. She would be placed on dialysis for the rest of her life if they decided not to end treatment. Corey didn't talk much about those last few days with her when the decision to end treatment was made. He told me he sat with her and sang; *his mother loved his voice.* Her death was very hard on Corey, and he never got over the fact that she wasn't able to meet the girls.

My dad had been updating the family on Corey's state, and I'm grateful for it. I've needed to process the information on my own, without having to be strong enough to pass along the updates to everyone else. As I stare down at his name in my phone, I realize this will be the first time I have spoken to him this weekend. *How am I going to face him? How do I tell my husband's father I don't think I can let the doctors keep tearing away at him?* No one and nothing can prepare you for a moment like this.

The line doesn't ring for more than five seconds before Ed answers.

"Dawn?" Concern radiates over the line.

I take a deep breath before answering. "Hi, Ed." My voice sounds heavy. I listen to it crack as my nerves overcome me.

"How are you? I've been thinking of you and the kids so much." His voice trembles with each word, but he remains calm.

I can't engage in conversation. My head falls into my hands, trying to blink back tears. My heart needs to prepare for grieving, and it's my personal

159

responsibility to take Corey out of his misery. Clearing my throat, I begin.

"Ed, I'm not sure what to do anymore. I don't think Corey is going to make it."

I pause to see if Ed has anything to say, and begin picking at my nails.

"They are beginning to remove some of his organs. No, not some, a lot. The prolonged loss of blood has caused them to fail, Ed. The doctors can continue to remove fragments of what remains or we can stop all medical care and let Corey pass away peacefully."

I swear I can hear the breath taken right out of Ed's body.

With a deep breath, I add, "I'm so sorry Ed, *so sorry*."

I can't imagine if someone called me to ask what to do for Thomas, Kristen, or Natalie. The knot in my stomach grows, and I can feel my body slowly start to overheat. *This is hard enough to live through; I don't need my mind wandering to other terrible scenarios.*

Ed clears his throat and begins to speak. "You know, I had to make this decision for Anne. It came down to the type of life I thought she would want to live."

I could feel the tears building up in my eyes. *Stay strong. You need to hold yourself together.*

He continues to speak, "It was the hardest decision of my life."

He understands the pain and the confusion I'm going through right now. Why didn't I call him sooner?

"You know Corey best, Dawn. You know that whatever decision you and the kids make we will support and understand."

The ball in my throat is growing larger with each tear I try to hold back. I try to remember their flight information. I believe they land at 2 PM today. *I can try to see if the doctors can keep him alive until then. How many more hours is that? It's about a quarter after four in the morning now. About ten more hours. No, I better say about twelve by the time they get their luggage and drive here. Could I ask the doctors to keep Corey in his misery for nearly another day?*

I can hear Ed blowing his nose in the background.

"I'm so sorry, Ed. I can't imagine Corey will make it until you get here, but I can ask if the doctors can try to keep him alive until you arrive." *Twelve hours is too long to hold on. It's twelve more hours in a coma for Corey and it's twelve more hours of agony for the kids and me.*

Ed doesn't hesitate with his response. "No. I can't let that happen." The sadness in his voice sends a shock wave through my body.

"I can put the phone up to his ear, if you want to talk to him?"

> *Thank God for technology.*

"That would be perfect, Dawn. Thank you."

Pushing off the floor, letting the coldness run from my fingertips through my body. Walking into the room I keep my head down.

I feel the tears finally release from my eyes as I lower the phone to Corey's ear. *I don't have to pretend to be strong for Ed anymore.* I can't imagine what Ed's telling his son for the very last time; I can't imagine speaking to one of my children for the very last time. *What would I say?* Glancing up, his lips catch my attention. The corner of his mouth is cracking from the dryness. My lungs feel tight and my breaths are short. Something about his lips looking as painful as they do. Something about realizing how a piece of him this small, so insignificant, has been abandoned. His lips were overlooked, but he depended on us. He will always depend on us if we keep interfering. **For everything.** Big or miniscule. *Even his chapped lips.* I turn to look at the floor; I can't look at Corey while he listens to his dad tell him goodbye.

| 4:29 AM |

Dawn

"Hello? Dawn?" Louise's voice sounds disoriented. I had a feeling she wasn't getting much sleep over the weekend, and she sounds terrible right now.

Corey and Louise have always been close, especially after their sister passed away. As Corey and Louise grew up, they remained just as close. They also had a weekly phone call on Saturday to catch up. Louise looks up to Corey, and telling her the news is sure to shatter her world.

"Louise, it isn't looking promising."
Her crying is loud and forceful; I can't make out any of her words. Losing *one* sibling was hard enough; now she is about to lose her *second* sibling, making her an only child, and she's only in her fifties. Taking a deep breath, I try to calm myself before going onward.

"Louise, I need to know if you would like me to hold the phone up to Corey."

I try to sound calm. I want to be strong for her during this terrible time.

"If you have any last words you want him to hear from you, I can bring him the phone."

Hearing his sister sob so violently is going to be hard for Corey to hear.

"No, no. I can't." She cries out on the phone.

Is she sure? Will she regret this?

"Are you sure?"

Should I give her some time to make sure this is what she really wants?

"Corey and I talk every week."

I can hear her sniffle as she realizes the weekly calls would soon

162

only be a memory.

"He knows how I feel about him and the relationship we have. I can't bear saying goodbye."

Each additional word is harder to understand as her sobs grow stronger once more.

"Plus it's not even Saturday; *we catch up on Saturdays.*"

- ELEVEN -

Dawn

The nurses begin to give me instructions, but I can barely hear them over my own thoughts. *Am I making the right decision? Is it time to let him go? Am I being a good wife? Have I been a good wife?*

"Ma'am, did you hear what I just said?"

Her head turns slightly when she asks her question. Each word slowly and carefully spoken.

Is it that obvious I'm not paying attention?

I look up at her with embarrassed, rosy cheeks. "Yes, I'm sorry. My thoughts got away from me."

"I understand. Well, like I said, we will disconnect the ventilator and slowly stop all IV treatment. We've turned off all monitors so you won't hear or see his vital signs. We'll be watching his vitals outside at the main desk. It won't be long after all treatments have been stopped."

Her eyes meet mine, and it's obvious she feels uncomfortable giving me a rundown on how my husband will shortly pass away.

"You may not be able to tell when he's passed, but when you hear a knock on the door you will know. We'll give you a few moments to get situated before we begin disconnecting. Let us know when you're ready."

Pausing once more, she interlocks her fingers and holds her hands in front of her.

"Take your time."

165

I nod my head to signal my understanding. My tears are all dried up and one last bit of strength enters my body. *I have to be strong for Corey right now. I want him to be completely at peace. I need to give him this moment; he of all people deserves a peaceful passing.* My brain is signaling to every muscle in my body to be still, be strong, and give every last bit of strength to Corey.

As I enter the room, it feels colder and darker inside. The loneliness is intensified now without the nurses running around. *The emptiness in the room matches the emptiness in my heart.* There's a small chair strategically placed right next to his bedside with a blanket draped along the back of it. The only light is coming from a dim five-foot floor lamp in the back corner. It's strange not having the green, blue, yellow, and red lights illuminating from his monitor.

I've already imagined what I'm going to do first. I walk over to Corey, and with each step I can feel my heart getting heavier, harder to carry. I stare at his lifeless body lying next to me. *How did it come to this, Corey?* I reach for his hand and gently lean down to plead to him, "Corey, if this isn't what you want, if there is anything you want me to do differently, please, I'm begging you, squeeze my hand, move your eyes, do *anything*, and I won't go forward with this."

I wait for what feels to be an eternity and wipe the tears rolling down my face before it hits the top of my lip. *As his wife, I have to honor him. I have to do what's best for him. I have to think about his well-being before mine.*

"Okay."

I nearly choke on the word.

I walk outside the room to notify the nurses to begin the disconnection process. As I turn to walk back in, I inhale a long, deep breath. *In a few minutes I will be a widow. I'll have lost the most important person in my life. Am I ready for this?*

I take each step inside a bit slower than the step before. *This room feels depressing; this can't be how Corey goes. Think.*

I reach for my phone and search Amazon music for 'Gospel Hymn Station.' Corey used to sing hymns all the time to put the kids to sleep. *I*

166

need to tell him how much I've enjoyed these past 28 years of marriage together. How grateful I am for all he's given the kids and me. How I have absolutely no idea how I'm going to survive without him.

"Corey, don't be afraid. You've done everything you've meant to do on this earth, and as much as we will miss you--*and damn*--will we miss you... "

The tears begin to cascade out of my eyes.

"...we know it's your time. It's time for you to join your mother and sister. It's time for you to watch over us from above. Don't stay in your pain for us; you've already done so much; *too much*, for us."

Did I tell him just how much I appreciate his support for me? Did I thank him enough times for the lifestyle he's provided for us?

"I hope you know how much I love you. Even with our arguments, I've never stopped loving you. You've had my heart from our first margaritas together. You've provided for our family better than anyone else. I hope…"

I've been an appreciative wife for all you've done for me. I have no idea what I'm going to do without you. I won't have someone to cook dinners for, or go on our planned retirement vacations with, or celebrate grandchildren with, or wake up next to every morning. I want you to stay here with me, be by my side when we celebrate our anniversary and our children's weddings. I want to buy our retirement home in Lake Keowee together like we've always dreamed about. I want to grow old with you Corey; I don't want to be a widow. I'm scared and I feel completely, utterly alone.

I'm holding onto his hand tightly, trying to hold back any more tears from falling. *You have to let him go, Dawn. You have to be strong and seem accepting of it or he won't leave. You're being selfish; he's in pain, let him go.* I can't speak anymore or I will get off track and tell him how much I can't imagine my life without him.

I hum along to the hymns playing and try to focus on my breathing.

"I love you more than you know, Corey; but we'll be okay."

|5:05 AM|

Dawn

Knock, knock.

My stomach drops and the noise frightens me. *That can't be the signal. I didn't even hear his breathing stop. Surely, I'd be able to notice a change in his breathing.* Guilt is slowly rising over my body. *How did I not know? Is it really all over?*

Two nurses walk in, but both avoid eye contact. I pull at the skin on my wrists trying to focus on something, anything else besides the guilt consuming me. One nurse listens to his heart and searches for his pulse. She seems so young. *This will be Kristen soon. Corey won't get to see her graduate from nursing school.*

"Time of death..."

Their voices leave my ears.

He barely survived twenty minutes without medical assistance. I hardly had any time alone with him.

Pausing to search for the positive, I look at the ground. *At least he barely suffered.* I can feel a sense of relief lift off of me. *This could have been a long, painful wait.* I look up at his face. *I hope you aren't disappointed in me.*

"Mrs. Owen, we are so very sorry for your loss."

Slowly redirecting my eyes to the nurses' voices, I can't even mutter a thank you. The words 'your loss' makes me want to throw up in the garbage bin next to me. I turn towards Corey. *I can't believe you're gone.*

Natalie

I wake up to a faint ringing in the background. *This again?*

Then I see the phone screen shining across the room with an incoming call from Mom. *Wrong ring.*

How long had we been asleep?! How could we fall asleep knowing Dad's time on earth is coming to an end? My mind is racing.

"Thomas your phone! Answer your phone! It's Mom!" I scream out.

He jolts off of the couch so quickly I can tell his vision blacks out because he's squeezing his eyes shut. Kristen is now opening her eyes with all of the commotion. Oakley, nestled on her stomach, jumps off the couch and bolts for Thomas. *Oakley knows something's wrong.* The neighbors have told us he hasn't eaten his food all weekend and he stays by the front door all day watching out the window, waiting for Mom and Dad to come home. Brandon's sitting up now, wrapping his arm around my shoulders. I let myself nudge my head under his chin. *I need all the protection I can get.* Every movement seems to be in slow motion.

"Mom?"

Thomas answers the call; he still seems disoriented but he's trying to focus.

"Hold on. I'm putting you on speaker."

His shaky hands bobble the phone ever so slightly. *Hurry up.*

"Okay, we're all listening."

Everyone's eyes are fixed on the iPhone. No one dares to breathe in fear of missing her next words.

"He just passed."

The room is silent. This is the first time I realize how cold the media room is; it feels so lonely even with everyone smashed together on the couch. My stomach starts cramping with nerves, I could barf. *What am I so nervous about?* My brain starts instantly reminding me of what his death really means for us. How our lives will be changed permanently. *How am I going to start my job without his advice? I didn't even get a chance to ask him what percentage to select for my 401K contributions. Who will I split the side of egg rolls with; everyone knows four is too many to eat alone. Who will take care of Mom? How will she afford anything-- the cars, the house?*

I can't form a tear; my nerves are overpowering any other feeling. This weekend has been a rollercoaster ride of emotions and when I really should be crying, I can't. *What kind of daughter doesn't cry when she learns of her dad's passing?* Now guilt is creeping up next to my nerves; making enough room for the two of them. The room starts to look like it's shrinking; I'm so small, so helpless without him. I know an anxiety attack is brewing. I turn to my siblings to try to focus on something else, to stop the attack from escalating. Kristen and Thomas are looking down at the floor. They are sitting still, not shedding a tear, not even blinking, just keeping silent. *Do they realize what this means too?*

Brandon breaks the silence, "I'm so sorry."

My eyes shift to him, but he's still focusing on the carpet. We all look as uncomfortable as we feel.

My attention reverts back to my mom in an attempt to calm down. "How are you getting home?" I ask her.

"I am going to Uber once I finish up here."

"No way! I'll come pick you up!" *Is she out of her mind?! There is no way I'm letting her sit in a 45-minute car ride with a stranger; alone in her thoughts.*

"I don't know how long I'll be here. The nurses mentioned some paperwork. You all need to sleep before Grandma and Grandpa O arrive."

She sounds firm in her decision, but I will try again anyway.

"Mom, please let me come get you. Brandon will come with me to keep each other awake."

As I try pleading with her, I realize how much I wish she was here with us. *She is all we have left. We need her.*

"No, Natalie. The nurses are calling me over; I should go. I love you."

She is so stubborn.

We all quietly echo back, "Love you too."

As Thomas ends the call, I reach for my phone and text Mom, "Please let me know when you get in the Uber. I'm waiting up for you."

Brandon readjusts to lie back down. He tugs at my arm to join him but I pull away. *I have to stay awake for my mom even if no one else does.* Thomas is still staring into the distance, and Kristen is texting someone on her phone. *Should we start updating the family? Is Grandpa telling everyone the news? Does Grandpa even know?* Mom didn't give us much information. I decide to text my boss. All I manage to type is "He has passed." *Hopefully he understands that means I won't be back in town for a few weeks.* Before I realize what I'm doing, I send the same text message to Brandon's mom. Brandon had been updating his family over the weekend, so this was the first text message she would receive from me. *Should I even be texting people? I'm not really sure who knows and who doesn't know. Everything has been happening so quickly.*

Thomas suddenly speaks out, still staring at the floor. "Me and Dad were supposed to go to the Vikings-Broncos game this year."

He still isn't crying. He looks emotionless and numb. The shock is setting in.

Dad was supposed to watch me start my first full-time job; he was supposed to be there to mentor me through it all.

Kristen looks up from her phone and joins in; "Dad was supposed to watch my pinning ceremony and my graduation from nursing school."

Dad was scheduled to be at my graduation in a month. He missed my undergraduate ceremony, but he promised to be at this one. He already booked his flight.

Thomas continues, "We all have tickets to go to the Wheels of Soul concert."

Dad was so excited because the concert included Tedeschi Trucks Band, Blackberry Smoke, and Shovels & Rope. I smile at the memory of my dad calling me when he bought the tickets. Tears fall onto my shirt knowing he no longer would be nudging us every five minutes to remind us to pay attention to their guitar skills.

Kristen can barely finish her sentence; her sobs have become too loud. "Can Mom afford the house payments?"

I'm going to vomit. The pit in my stomach comes back. I crawl over to her side of the couch and embrace her. *I wish I could tell her it's going to be okay. We would support Mom; help her with the payments and start repaying her for everything the two of them have given us.* But I don't utter a word because I know it isn't true. I haven't even started my job. Kristen still has a semester left of school. Thomas has his own monthly mortgage and personal expenses to cover. *More importantly, who is going to be her person? Who will be the one to listen to her vent about the stress we cause her? Hold her hand when she is ready to break? Kiss her goodnight? How are we going to do this?*

The silence in the room returns; no one says anything because no one has anything to say to make each other feel better. No words could take away this pain.

Snuggling next to Kristen, she whispers, "Dad was supposed to walk us down the aisle."

Her glossy eyes turn to me before she finishes her thought.

"Dance with you to Tim McGraw's song and with me to Chuck Wicks'."

Brandon had not received permission from my dad yet. Kristen's future husband will never get the chance to meet my dad. How is this supposed to be the plan?

All I manage to respond with is, "I know."

The happiest day of a girl's life would now be filled with tears and sadness. I can't imagine ever getting married now. I can't imagine doing anything anymore.

| 5:22 AM |

<u>Dawn</u>

I walk over to the nurses as I finish updating my parents of Corey's passing. I can feel the adrenaline leave my body and I realize how exhausted I really am.

"Mrs. Owen, we have a few questions for you whenever you're ready."

Let's get this over with. I just want to go home.

I respond, "Okay" to indicate I'm ready to begin now.

"First, we need to know if you want an autopsy done on your husband?"

My eyes narrow while my fingers curl into a fist. *I can't believe she is asking me this right now. Haven't you cut him open enough?? You removed half of his organs! What more do you need to see? We know he died from internal bleeding. Remember, no one could properly stop it??* My arms land folded across my chest.

"Absolutely not." My voice sounds harsh, but I can't help it. *How could I let them cut him open anymore? No more procedures and definitely no more removing or moving around organs. He's at peace now; his body should be, too.*

"Okay, can you please sign here…"

Stacks of papers are pushed towards my chest, and a pen dangling from the clipboard by a metal, string pen holder.

"…confirming you have declined an autopsy?"

My eyes are so tired and dry. Everything looks fuzzy; I can barely make out which line I should be signing.

"Great, thank you."

It's obvious this nurse has done this paperwork routine before.

"Next, I need to know what funeral home you will be using."

Shit. I haven't even thought that far ahead. As of six hours ago, I wasn't sure if he was going to make it out of here or not. We have only lived in Charlotte for four years, and getting ourselves acquainted with a funeral home wasn't a thought for us.

My eyes pacing back and forth, I respond, "Um, I haven't really thought that far."

"That's totally okay. We can place him in the morgue until you decide."

My stomach begins to flip when I imagine Corey being placed there. *There is no way in hell I would let him rest in a morgue.*

"No, no."

Shaking my head, I try to think.

"Give me five minutes. I will give you the name of a funeral home in five minutes."

I step away and look through my contacts. I'm trying to think of someone, anyone, who would know local funeral homes. I land on Carrie. Her mother had recently passed away and I remember her explaining how wonderful the funeral home was who handled her mother's services. I glance at my watch; it's only half past five in the morning on a Sunday. *I am definitely going to wake her up.*

The rings sound long and slow as each one goes unanswered. *Please Carrie, please.*

Finally on the fourth ring, she answers. "Dawn?"

Her voice is sleepy and she sounds confused.

Another person I'm telling for the first time. My throat feels scratchy and I dread telling her the news. *I better get used to this.*

"Hi, Carrie. I'm so sorry to wake you. What was the funeral home you used for your mom again?"

Maybe she won't even wonder why I'm asking.

"Heritage Homes. Why? Is everything okay?"

I can hear her readjusting herself in bed as she slowly wakes up.

"Corey has…"

I can't finish the sentence. I can't imagine reciting this over and over again to people. My head feels like it's spinning with every tear. *I'm losing control.*

"Dawn, where are you? I'm coming to you."

Pull yourself together, Dawn. You need to be strong. You can't be waking people up at five in the morning and have them running to you.

"No, I just needed the name of the funeral home. Please stay where you are."

My fingers rest on the wall, trying to push off of it for strength.

"I'll call you later today with more information. Thanks though."

I end the call before she has a chance to argue.

Heritage Homes. I guess this will be the funeral home. What other choice do I have?

I lock my phone and shovel it in my pocket. Turning back around, I approach the nurse again. "Heritage Homes will be the funeral home."

"Okay then."

She is feverishly writing down information. *She's a talented nurse. She is able to separate her heart from her work.*

"That's all we need for now. We will contact the funeral home to make

175

arrangements to transport Corey. Again…"

Her voice trails off as she lifts her eyes from her paperwork to meet mine.

"I'm so sorry about your loss."

She seems genuine. *Maybe she isn't so good at separating her emotions from her work after all.*

"Thank you."

I open the Uber app and type in my requested address, home. 15 minutes till Aaron will arrive at the main hospital entrance.

I begin to walk down the hallway to exit the ICU unit, and I finally notice how lonely this hallway feels. They keep the unit dark and gloomy. I look around and there isn't anyone in sight. The hall is quiet; every step I take sounds piercing. I feel completely alone in this hallway.

"Mrs. Owen?!" someone calls out.

Finally, someone's steps sound louder than mine. I don't even turn around. I simply stop and wait for them to reach me. This time it's a new nurse. I vaguely remember her face but I can't remember her role-- *maybe the dialysis nurse?*

"We created these for your family. I know it isn't much but I hope it can provide some comfort."

She hands me over a bag and it takes my eyes a second to focus on what it is. The bag contains four small vials with a small paper copy of Corey's three final heartbeats. *I'm holding the last piece we have of him.* My eyes fill with tears and I keep walking towards the main entrance of the hospital. *This is all I have of him anymore.* The vials are tightly held near my heart as I walk out of the ICU unit.

- TWELVE -

Dawn

The air outside is crisp. *I wish I had a jacket right now.* I peek down at my phone to check Aaron's location. *Why does it look like he is moving away from me?* I hit the contact button and give him a call.

"Hello?" His voice is deep.

He seems irritated.

"Hi. This is Dawn, your pick up. I was wondering where you are because it looks like you're driving away from me."

"I just came to the entrance, you weren't there, ma'am. I'm canceling the ride."

What the hell! I have been standing here for nearly fifteen minutes!

"What? I've been outside the whole time. I never saw you drive up." I try to keep my voice composed.

"I did. It'll only be a $5 charge and you can request someone else when you're ready."

Now I can feel my blood starting to boil. *There is not a chance I'm waiting for another fifteen minutes for a new driver, plus being charged for a cancellation. Of course this is happening right now. I should've just had someone pick me up.*

"Sir, can you please turn around? I'm at the main entrance. I promise you I didn't see your car. I'm exhausted and I really just want to get home."

Can't he see he's picking me up from a hospital? I've had a long freaking night. Just pick me up.

177

He pauses before answering, *weighing out his options, I suppose*. "I'll come one more time but if I come back and you're not there, I'm canceling the ride."

I end the call. *What an asshole*. I cross my arms over my chest and wait for his stupid, black Honda. *I know I shouldn't be so irritated; I should know the importance of not jumping to conclusions. Maybe he's having just as crappy of a morning as I am*. I start to calm myself down as his car turns the corner.

I open the door and greet him. "Thanks for coming back."

He doesn't answer me. It's quite obvious he's annoyed with me. I try to ignore the awkward silence while he pulls out of the entrance.

"Look, I'm sorry if I missed you the first time."

Now I'm starting to feel guilty. *Who knows what happened to him this morning.*

"It's all good." His response lightens the tension in the car.

"How are you doing this morning?"

Why does it always feel necessary to engage in small talk during Uber drives? Maybe I'm just trying to distract myself from reality. Maybe we all are.

"Just a busy morning with the kids. Trying to get some work in before church."

I knew he would have a backstory. I bet his kids made him late this morning and it put him in a bad mood.

"How about you? Leaving the hospital pretty early?"

"Yeah, my husband just passed away."

What the hell are you saying, Dawn?! Why would you tell this stranger such personal information? More importantly, why does your voice sound like you were simply commenting on the weather? What's wrong with you?

The awkwardness in the car slowly creeps its way back in. *Great job, Dawn.*

"Wow. I'm so, I'm so sorry to hear that." It's apparent he feels uncomfortable.

Is this how it's always going to be when I tell people?

We didn't speak for the rest of the car ride.

I swear I didn't blink before we're suddenly pulling into my driveway. I'm exhausted; I didn't have the energy to let my mind wander during the drive.

"Thank you again."

The door almost closes before I hear Aaron say, "Have a blessed Sunday. I'll be praying for you and your family."

My heart aches as he says it. *I can't believe I'm the person strangers offer prayers to.* I shut the car door and walk towards the front door. I can feel the exhaustion setting in as I walk up the front steps. I grab the side rails to help me up. When I finally approach the door, the knob is locked. *How fitting.* I don't have the energy to be upset; I head back down the stairs and go to the garage keypad. *Why didn't I start here?*

When I finally enter the house, I freeze in the kitchen. My house doesn't feel the same. It's like I'm walking into it for the first time; nothing looks familiar. I see Corey's work computer and briefcase sitting on the kitchen table. As I walk over to tidy up his paperwork, I begin to envision Corey on Friday. *He had a meeting that morning; he probably took the call right here. He sat in this chair.* My fingers trace over his notes, allowing myself to half-heartedly smile. His handwriting is horrific, but it brings me comfort looking at it right now. I dread my bedroom, but I know I need sleep.

I stand outside the door frame as I peer into the room. The sheets are ruffled. *They were never made Friday morning.* He never had a chance to make it. Everything escalated too quickly. I remember back to the ambulance call. *Corey was in bed when the EMTs arrived, wasn't he? Did he not feel good and go back to bed?* I try to piece the puzzle together. *Where did he throw up the blood?* I race to the bathroom, but there are no signs of blood anywhere. *Did someone come clean up?* I catch his side of the bathroom out of the corner of my eyes. His toothbrush and contact case sit untouched. I walk over to his comb sitting out on the counter; I slowly pick it up and grip it tightly. *I want to feel him, his presence.* Bringing it back down, I open the drawer and put it away. *Why am I tidying up? It's pointless. This stuff is useless.* I need both of my hands on the counter to stop myself from falling down. I look up to the mirror and realize it's the first time I'm seeing myself since Friday. *I look like shit.* My hair's a mess and my makeup's completely smeared. *I guess I've been looking as bad as I feel.* At that moment, I let go of everything I've been trying so desperately to hold in. My sobs are loud. I can feel each one travel all the way through my body and pull in my stomach as I struggle for a breath in between each cry. My fingers frantically try to stop each tear from coming out. *I can't wake the kids up. I need to go to bed.* I walk away, weaker than I was before.

As I reach my bed, my body completely collapses. The mattress feels cold and the room feels empty. *This is the loneliest I have ever felt in my entire life.* A king bed feels so unnecessary for one person. *I already miss you so much, Corey. How am I going to make it through every night alone?*

| 7:29 AM |

<u>Natalie</u>

My eyes abruptly open and I'm suddenly wide awake. *Crap! I fell asleep!*

I jump off the couch and race downstairs. The kitchen clock reads 7:29 AM. *Mom! Did she ever make it home?*

I'm calling out, "Mom!" before I make it to her room.

She flips over and jolts up. "Yes? Natalie? Is everything okay?" She sounds as scared as I do.

Oh thank goodness. She finally made it home; we need her.

"Yes, everything's okay. I'm so glad you're home. I'm so, so sorry I fell asleep."

I begin to cry as I say it out loud. *I've let her down. I've let down Dad. I should've been there when she walked inside. I needed to be there to tell her how my heart aches for her right now. I was supposed to be there to tell her we will figure out the next steps together, and how I'll do anything to help her. But instead, I'm two hours too late and I've woken her up from her first deep sleep in days. I'll never forgive myself for this.*

"Oh, honey. Don't cry. I'm glad you were sleeping."

I crawl into her bed and give her a hug. *I've missed her so much.*

She speaks before I get a chance. "Let's get some sleep."

We both get situated in the bed, staring at opposite walls. I feel so out of place in this room, but I know I need to be here for my mom. She keeps tossing and turning. *She can't fall asleep either.*

"Mom? Are you awake?" I whisper, in case I'm wrong and she is sleeping.

She turns over as she answers, "Yeah."

"Do you think Dad knew he was dying?"

I couldn't let this thought go. I need to know if there were any signs that he was afraid.

Dawn

I answer immediately without giving the question much thought, "No, I don't think so. Do you?"

"I'm not sure how that works."

Why does she sound like a young girl trying to find answers to the mystery of life?

She rolls back over. *I guess that was all she needed to hear.*

I start analyzing her question. *Did he know? I don't think so. He never mentioned anything, but why would he?* I think back to the past few months.

We always had the goal of going to all fifty states together, and we promised to keep Alaska as the final state we would conquer together. Yet, last May he begged to break the promise. He wanted to take the entire family on an

181

extravagant cruise leaving from Seattle. I kept resisting, reminding him we still had kids in college. When I finally agreed to the idea, he kept pushing to do the most grandiose excursions. "We have to go dog sledding because Kristen loves dogs." "We have to go on the floatplane because it's the best way to spot wildlife, and Thomas wants to see a bear." "We have to take a helicopter to a glacier because Natalie loves those Planet Earth documentaries." "We have to do the ATV ride, just because it's an ATV ride." It was the vacation of a lifetime, and he didn't want to hold back on anything.

Later that month, Thomas, Corey, and I went back to our old town, Nazareth. Thomas' childhood friend was getting married, and we had received an invitation to attend. Our visit brought back many memories, and reminiscing with old friends was the highlight of the trip. I make a mental note to find the photo booth pictures of us dressed up in masks and Mardi Gras beads.

Then, in July, he rented a house on Lake Keowee for the 4th. He also rented a speedboat and every accessory possible. We had tubing, water-skiing, and wakeboarding. I close my eyes and imagine the smile on his face when Kristen and Natalie bounced up and down on the tubes. Corey drove the boat and found sandbars to anchor to so we could grill. On the final day, Corey extended the speedboat rental because the kids were having so much fun. He never thought twice about the price when it was spent on making family memories.

I remember I was worried about how much he was traveling in August and September, but he assured me it was all necessary trips.

In the beginning of August, he surprised his sister by flying into Grand Junction. His dad was visiting her, and he wanted to surprise them both. He talked about the looks on their faces for weeks.

Corey hadn't been back home to Montana in a while, and his dad's brother was celebrating his 90th birthday at the end of August. A number of his extended family would be there, some of them Corey hadn't seen in over a decade. Of course, Corey waited until the last minute to book his flight, and the ticket was over $600. I remember telling him that was an absurd amount of money to pay for an airline ticket, but he insisted. *Thank God he went.*

Two weeks later, he and Thomas went to the Packers-Vikings game and then the following weekend he was in Vegas to see the Queen concert with friends. I could tell he was exhausted from the trips, but he never complained; he made sure everyone was enjoying themselves.

For Thanksgiving, we hosted my family. We had beautiful weather. I'll never forget the corn-hole tournament Corey and I won. We stayed in pajamas all day and danced to Meatloaf songs. The embarrassment on the kid's faces was priceless and only encouraged Corey to keep dancing.

For Christmas, Corey rented a house on Lake Lure in the mountains of Asheville big enough to host his family. The house came with a pontoon boat; we floated around the lake with hot cocoa for everyone. We had Biltmore House Christmas tickets and made reservations in the famous stable for dinner.

We'll be forever grateful for having the last two holidays with both of our families.

The more I think back, Corey did more in this past year than ever before. He was reaching out to family members he hadn't seen in years. He took advantage of seeing old friends. We made some of our best family memories in the past year. *How did this all align so perfectly? Did he have some inclination to make the most of the prior year?*

What am I thinking right now? I shake my head in disbelief. *Of course he didn't know; I'm just extremely sleep deprived.*

- THIRTEEN -

Kristen

As I open my eyes, I peek at the media room and quickly shut my eyes again. *I don't want to wake up to this; I don't want any of it to be true.*

Brandon's cough forces me to open my eyes again.

"Hey Kristen, you awake?" He whispers.

I guess so.

I mumble back, "Yeah."

"Do you know what time your grandparents land? I'll pick them up so you can all stay together."

Thank God Brandon is here. The airport drive is miserable; it's not overly far but just long enough to make it a nuisance.

"Um, let me check. They texted us their flight info yesterday."

My phone screen lights up, indicating that I have several notifications. I scroll past the Snapchat and Instagram alerts. *How can I possibly respond to my friends right now?* The Niners Outlook alert, the school's notification system, catches my attention. *My professor must have responded to my email early this morning.* My heart feels like it's in my stomach. *Is she okay with me missing some school?* Last I emailed her, Dad was still alive.

I quickly maneuver to the group message with my grandparents and aunt.

"2 PM. They land at 2 PM." I don't want to open the email in front of Brandon.

"Ok, thanks. I'm gonna go start the coffee pot for everyone. Want me to bring you up a cup?"

185

Is it that obvious I want him to leave? That I need a moment alone? I glance over to Thomas, still sound asleep on the opposite side of the couch; *at least I have a moment in a room where I'm the only one awake.* It finally registers that Natalie isn't here anymore. *Did she already get up?*

"Sure. Thanks."

After I watch him leave the room, I refocus my attention to my phone. Before I hit 'open,' I glance over to make sure Thomas is still sleeping. *I don't want everyone thinking I need to be comforted every time I cry or have a moment of weakness.* With Thomas still out cold, I open the email.

"Kristen,

I'm so sorry to hear about your dad. Please do not worry about classwork. Take care of yourself and your family for now.

We can discuss a plan when your dad gets out of ICU. I'll be praying for you and your family.

Dr. Murphy."

It feels like someone has punched me right in the gut and knocked the wind right out of me. I could almost laugh at the words, but my eyes start to fill with tears. I turn my direction to the ceiling. *I should've never emailed her yesterday. I should've waited until Sunday to do an update. Now I get to correct myself and tell her that her prayers are too late.* I want to smash my phone against the wall. *I'm so dumb. I should've known the prognosis didn't look good. I shouldn't have been so hopeful.* I bury my head into my hands and quietly let go of the tears built up in my eyes. *How am I supposed to go back to school? I'll never be able to focus again. I'll never be able to get through my last two semesters. What's the point in any of this anymore? I couldn't even recognize the severity of my dad's situation; I can't be a nurse. I don't deserve to be a nurse.*

Dawn

I feel better even after only two hours of sleep. I know I won't be able to sleep any longer; my mind is racing with things that need to get done today. Natalie is still sleeping. *I'm glad she came downstairs earlier; the room feels a little less intimidating with someone beside me.* I turn to the clock and notice it's just past 9 AM. *You need to get this over with before starting anything else. They deserve to know before others.*

I cautiously leave the bed in an attempt not to wake Natalie up. Once I successfully get out, I grab my phone and head to my bathroom.

The tile feels cold on my feet, but I don't mind. It helps me focus on the tile rather than what I'm about to do. I'm staring at Jess' number in my contact book. *Stay calm, Dawn. They will know what to do. They need to know first.*

Corey worked with Evan for several years at his previous company. When Evan became the CEO of the new company, he asked Corey to join the team. Evan and his wife, Jess, have been there for Corey and me every moment since we left Pennsylvania. They made Charlotte feel like our home, and I appreciated their friendship. Probably more than they really know.

I press her number before I have another second to delay the call. The rings are long and loud. The call goes to voicemail. I remember their family is traveling back from Iceland today. *I better not ruin the end of their trip. Maybe I should call tomorrow?*

My phone pings with a text from Jess almost immediately after I hang up.

"You're supposed to be in church right now. Guessing it was a butt dial?"

I could've made church this morning. I can still make church this afternoon. But I know I'm not going. I need to be here with my kids and, for the first time, it doesn't feel necessary to go to church.

I text her back, "no. need you and Evan to call me when you have a chance."

I'm sure this text message will catch her off guard. *What could I possibly need*

187

this early on a Sunday?

She calls me almost instantly after I send her the text message. I don't let the first ring finish before I answer.

She speaks before I get a chance. "Is everything okay?"

My voice cracks and I start to whimper. "No, Jess. It isn't. Are you with Evan?"

"No. What's going on, Dawn?"

The panic in her voice is overwhelming. My vision is tunneling.

"I need you to go get him, Jess."

I want to tell them both at the same time. I want to limit the number of times I have to say it out loud. The silence is brief while I wait for Jess to get Evan.

"Okay, he's right here. It's on speaker. What's happening?"

Her words sound rushed.

"You're scaring me…"

"Corey…" I have to take a breath before I finish.

The bathroom door opens and Natalie is standing at the entrance. The edges of my mouth rise as I give her a look of gratitude. She looks half asleep, but she sits down on the floor next to me and places her hand over top of mine. Her presence gives me strength. Just being here for me, not saying a word, just sitting next to me is what I need.

"Corey has passed away."

The line is silent. *I guess I should've warned them or gave them a heads up before blurting it out.* I can't imagine the shock. It's not as if Corey was sick. There were no signs or symptoms leading up to this moment. *Or were there and I missed them?* Either way, this shouldn't be the news I'm telling them on a Sunday morning.

"What?" Jess finally asks, completely shocked. "How?"

"He was bleeding internally and there was nothing the doctors could do to stop it."

Natalie squeezes my hand, reminding me I'm not in this alone.

"It happened so fast. He was admitted Friday and passed away this morning."

More silence.

"I'm so sorry, Dawn. For you, for the kids, for everyone."

Jess is still the only one talking.

"I, I really don't know what to say."

Did Evan hear me? What's he thinking? What's he doing? The two of them share a love for music. Evan and Corey play music together frequently with friends. *Did he realize this meant he would need to find a new guitar player for their small 3-person band?*

"It still doesn't quite feel real."

I let out a weep and continue my sentence.

"I wanted to tell you first so Evan could be the one to tell the staff."

"Who knows?"

Still only Jess talking.

"No one besides family."

"Evan will address it Monday. Today, focus on your family. Don't worry about telling people; we can help you. We'll help with whatever you need."

I can hear the sincerity echo in each word.

"Thank you, Jess. I better go see if my kids are awake."

I glance over at Natalie who is staring out into the distance. I can't tell if she's listening anymore or lost in her thoughts.

"Of course. Let us know if you need anything. Anything Dawn. Really. I'm *so* sorry again to hear this. We love you."

Her support means the world to me. I knew she would know what to do. As I hang up, I turn to Natalie.

"You okay, honey?"

What a dumb question, Dawn.

She still doesn't make eye contact with me, but whispers, "Are *you* going to be okay, Mom?"

I feel a tug at my heart. *What a loaded question. How do I answer that?* I want to sob into her shoulder and tell her I have no idea what's going to happen, tell her how scared I am, tell her how alone I feel, but I know I have to be strong.

She turns her head and looks directly at me. I can tell she's trying to search for truth in my eyes when she rephrases her question. "I mean, will you be okay financially?"

Of course she would be thinking about logistics. Emotionally, she knew none of us were going to be okay. At least not for a while.

She's analyzing my every move. Waiting to see if I show any signs of lying or hesitation in my response. There's no point in trying to sugarcoat anything to her. "I'm really not sure." *Corey always took care of the financial planning.*

Worry is growing on her face.

"I'll make it work either way. I can get a job. It'll be okay. Please don't worry."

She turns her attention back to the tile, and her head falls lower than before. *I need to assure her I will be okay. I can't have my kids worrying about me; I should be the one worrying about them.*

I grab her hand and say, "Lets go get some coffee. It'll be easier to plan a to-do list with a fresh cup of coffee." I shoot her a smile as she turns back

190

towards me, but she doesn't seem to notice. She's still trying to search for certainty in my eyes. *She knows I'm not as strong as I'm acting.*

Thomas

The noises downstairs wake me up. I scan the empty media room; *I guess I'm the last one to get up.*

As I'm walking down the stairs, I hear Mom and Kristen talking about cancelling something but I can't make out what it is. I see Natalie sitting at the kitchen island with Brandon. Both are silently drinking their coffee, not uttering a word to one another, not looking up at each other.

When I make it into the kitchen, Mom turns to me. "Good morning, Bud. How did you sleep?"

The question sounds ridiculous as she says it, but I know she's trying to normalize the morning.

"Fine."

Rubbing my eyes, I try to make out the food on the counter.

"You?"

Ah, muffins.

She jumps into today's plan without answering the question. "Brandon is going to pick up Grandma and Grandpa O. from the airport so we can all stay here. We should probably talk about a few things before everyone gets here."

The scratching on the door interrupts her. We all turn our attention to the front door. Oakley is scratching at it. He's waiting for Dad to come home.

191

I yell out in a pleading voice, "Come here, Oakley."

He turns to look at me but then returns to scratching at the door.

"Come here, bud." I hit my hand on my thigh, hoping it'll help change his mind.

He looks out the window one more time before turning to slowly walk towards me. His eyes look droopy, and he barely lifts his head up to look at me. I sit down on the floor and begin petting behind his ears. This usually calms him down when he gets anxious from too many people being in the house. *Hopefully it will work now, too.*

Mom continues, "I'm going to go call Blumenthal to see if we can turn in our tickets for tonight and then we can discuss some important details as a family."

That's what they were cancelling. I forgot they had tickets to Dear Evan Hansen tonight. Kristen has wanted to see this play for forever. *Dad would be upset if he knew plans were being canceled.*

Oakley leaves me and walks into the living room. He jumps in Dad's chair. The chair where he sat to watch Vikings games, where he would play hours of Candy Crush, where he would strum the guitar for all of us. Oakley isn't allowed on furniture, but no one yells at him to get off. Oakley wants Dad to come home. *We all do.*

| 12:43 PM |

Dawn

No one has said much to each other, and there are only so many generic questions I can ask about lunch. *I want to talk to the kids about this week before everyone gets here. I need a moment alone to figure out what's best for us without a hundred different opinions circling around us. What I need to talk about needs to be done with my kids only.*

192

When Brandon leaves for the airport, I decide to call everyone to the living room. *This is our chance. The details of the upcoming days are the one piece I can control and it will keep me centered and focused. I need this.*

"I know this is tough for everyone."

All three sets of their eyes look glossy; they're fighting to hold in their tears.

"We need to be there for each other. Especially this week."

Kristen wipes her check with her sleeve, Natalie won't make eye contact, and Thomas has his arms crossed. We all feel and look uncomfortable. *How can I make this better?*

Since no one chimes in, I continue. "I also think we need to discuss the upcoming week. Because Natalie and Kristen are still in school, I think we need to try to have the funeral arranged as soon as possible."

Natalie gets up from her chair. *Where is she going? We have to talk about this.* When she returns from the direction of the linen closet, she has a box of tissues. She takes a tissue for herself before giving the box to Kristen.

"The funeral home should be calling me tomorrow to discuss options."

Still, no one is answering me. *Should I not be pushing this right now? Am I making the wrong decision? The kids are obviously hurting too badly to talk about this right now. What am I thinking?*

Finally Thomas breaks the silence. "I asked the manager on my project to give me a call later today. I'm going to see if I can take off this week from work."

Natalie adds, "I texted my boss this morning letting him know about…it."

No one wants to say what "it" is out loud.

She continues, "He said to stay at home as long as I need to, and he would talk to the director of my program about taking a week off from school."

Realization comes over me that maybe my kids aren't so little anymore. *Maybe they don't need to be told what the next steps would be. Maybe I would need them to help me more than the reverse.*

I look to Kristen, waiting for her response. "I haven't responded to my professors yet, but I will. I'm sure they'll be fine with me staying home for a few days. I told a classmate and she said she would send me anything I miss."

A sense of relief comes over me. *Thank God my kids can stay here with me. We need each other.*

I continue to go over details. "The other thing I want you all to start thinking about is whether we want to do a burial or cremation."

I watch each one of them cringe when I ask the question.

"I know it's incredibly hard to think about, but Dad never specified and I want us to have our thoughts organized before everyone arrives."

Kristen looks up and gently adds. "If we bury him, where would it be? Montana? Colorado? Pennsylvania? Here?"

She pauses in between each option, testing if any of them sound like the right decision.

I haven't thought that far. *We didn't live here long enough to really establish a strong tie, and what if the kids move? What if I move?* My stomach turns at the thought of his grave going unattended.

Thomas speaks up. "Should he be buried next to his mom and sister?"

Kristen's response is soft and quiet. "But then we would barely see him. And what if we have a bad day and want to talk to him?"

Now my stomach is completely in knots with the thought of not being able to see him whenever I need him, whenever I'm confused or frustrated with parenthood.

I decide to speak up. "Well, what about cremation? We could each have a piece of him just in case we ever move away."

194

The silence consumes the room as the kids think about the option.

Natalie groans, "Ugh, but the thought of the process makes me want to vomit. Aren't their bodies set on fire?"

Thomas looks at her and adds, "But it isn't his body anymore. You can't think of it that way; plus it's way more sophisticated than that."

"I like the idea of everyone having his ashes."

Kristen finally raises her eyes when she joins in.

"When we each have our own places, we'll still have Dad with us."

I take a look around the living room and into the kitchen. *This house will feel enormous with everyone gone.* I shake these thoughts and return to the conversation.

"I agree, cremation is probably the best option for our family. We'll get Grandpa O. and Aunt Louise's thoughts when they arrive."

One item checked off my to-do list.

"Also, for the next few days, I want everyone to think about the funeral. Consider if you want to speak or don't want to speak. We don't have to make this decision right now, but I want everyone to be thinking about it."

What am I thinking? Do I want to speak? I'm not sure I can; what would I even say? Who would I be talking to? I don't even know who's going to come.

I place a small notepad and a pen on the coffee table before leaving the living room.

"I'm leaving this here for anyone to write down any questions, concerns, or thoughts for the week."

I pray my children don't feel alone or afraid to speak up. With a heavy heart, I leave the room and hope my kids know I'm trying my best.

| 3:07 PM |

Natalie

Everyone has dissipated into different rooms. I keep myself busy by checking Brandon's location. *I'm surprised how much I miss him right now.*

When he's finally five minutes away, I let everyone know. My hands are clammy and my stomach is uneasy. I've been so excited for Brandon to come back. I didn't realize how nervous I was to see Dad's family. *Their pain is so different.* They are now losing their only son and their only brother. The thoughts intensify the anxiousness I feel in the room.

I hear the door open and suitcases nicking the walls. The dogs barking add to the commotion. I hear Brandon telling them he can take their suitcases to their rooms upstairs. *I can't face them; I'm not strong enough to see their faces.*

I listen to Thomas and Kristen greet them at the door. I hear some sniffling and it only makes me dread coming out of my room more.

As I turn the corner into the kitchen, my eyes meet my grandpa's first. Every part of his body looks in pain. He looks like he's aged about ten years. *Heartache is a son of a bitch.* I walk over to embrace him. With my arms wrapped around him, he whispers, "I'm so sorry, Nattie." His arms feel like my dad and his voice sounds like his voice, too. Hearing the nickname my dad gave me when I was little makes me tense up. I can't manage to say, "So am I." Tears form in my eyes, and I know I won't be able to hold it in. I close my eyes to avoid watching the world around me shatter into pieces.

The moment he loosens his grip, I notice a rivulet of tears running down his face. He reaches for his handkerchief in his breast pocket. I've never seen my grandpa cry before and my sadness shifts to him. *No one should ever have to bury their child, especially twice.*

Kristen

The energy in the house keeps shifting. It brings comfort being surrounded by those you love the most; yet, at the same time, it brings discomfort. The constant flow of people, unanswered phone calls, and dinners piling up on our porch reminds me of what brought us to this point. My dad has passed and no chicken enchilada dish can fill the hole in my heart, no matter how much it tries.

The living room discussions remain light and meaningless. Both sets of grandparents are chatting and discussing the changes in the Montana weather. My aunt and sister are talking about school and her excitement about graduating soon. Uncle Danny, Thomas, and Brandon are talking about some recent mountain biking trip. *How, in a room full of people, do I feel so isolated, so lonely?*

Mom's bedroom door opens and she walks into the living room. Her reading glasses on top of her head force a few pieces of hair to fall out of place. She has several crinkled papers in her hands and the circles under her eyes are dark. She's been in her room for hours now. She wanted to be prepared when the funeral home calls tomorrow so she'd been working on Dad's obituary. No one stopped her when she told us she needed to work on it. Her to-do lists have always been a coping method for her. Whether it be packing for a vacation or college dorm move-ins, she always has her list to help her stay in control of the situation.

Standing in front of the fireplace, she clears her throat in an attempt to gather attention.

"I've finished the obituary."

The talking in the room comes to a hush and all eyes turn to her. She seems nervous and vulnerable. *Has she forgotten she's reading this in front of her family, not strangers in a poetry café?*

As she begins to read, people start cutting in. I can't make out who is saying what or what grammatical error is being corrected. My eyes are focused on my mom. Each critique is slowly weakening her. But she tries to stay poised, and makes adjustments with her blue pen. I want to tell her how proud I am of her; tell her how impressive it is that she was able to do this right now, but I keep my mouth shut. I let the adjustments continue even when I can feel my voice itching to stop it. When she finishes, she opens the floor for comments and opinions. *It's wonderful and well-written. It shows a glimpse into the person Dad was, and it portrays the legacy we need to build upon.* When the opinions start flowing, I watch her body lose its posture and her spine curl up after her head falls down as she searches for a chair to sit down to make more edits. She's defeated. *Am I the only one who can see the small tear falling from her eyes?* Before she makes it to the chair, the papers drop and the pen hits the floor.

"I can't do this anymore. You write it and I'll read over it tomorrow."

Her voice sounds angry and defeated. She isn't putting up a fight anymore. I watch her turn away from us and slam the bedroom door behind her. Natalie chases after her. I turn my head back to the living room. All of the people we love the most are all sitting wide-eyed and confused. *I know everyone is trying to help; we all want the best obituary for Dad.* But Mom needs support and reassurance that her work is good enough. The division is apparent, and in some ways warranted, but not what we need right now. *How can I fix this? Can I fix this?*

Part IV

MONDAY

MARCH 25TH

- FOURTEEN -

Dawn

I listen to Kristen snoring on the air mattress below my bed. Natalie stopped tossing and turning about forty minutes ago, so I assume she finally fell asleep. *I wish I could go to sleep.* My mind struggles to turn off the guilt. *Did I miss something Friday morning?* I try to replay the morning, but I can barely remember anything. I don't know if I've subconsciously blacked out the memories of the weekend or if I'm too tired to think a few days back. I search through my phone for answers. *Did Corey ever text me saying he was having stomach pain last week?* I can't find anything. *Did he tell anyone he was feeling sick?* I quietly open the drawer of the nightstand next to me. Before reaching in, I look around to make sure I didn't wake the girls up.

I reach for his phone. I haven't had the courage to look at his phone yet. I'm terrified I'm going to find the sign I missed and realize this whole situation is my fault. *I'd never forgive myself; my kids would never forgive me.* As I hit the home screen, a text notification makes me lose my breath. It's from Natalie. She texted him Friday telling him that she was thinking of him. I double-check the time of the message, and the flashback of Corey being restrained and intubated hits me. *He never saw her text message; this would kill Natalie if she ever found out she was too late.* My throat is too tight to continue looking at missed text messages. I go back to his homepage and see three red notifications on his calendar. I assumed it was going to be work meetings, but I almost choke on my surprise when I see its reminders of dentist and doctor appointments for the upcoming week. *He was supposed to get his cast off this week.* I make a mental note to add notifying the health care offices of his passing to my to-do list. *What else do I need to cancel?* I think about the upcoming weeks and all the plans we've made. The concerts we have tickets to, the airfare to go to Natalie's graduation, the 4th of July trip to Lake Keowee. *I can't imagine doing any of this without him. I don't want to do any of this without him.* I place the phone back into the drawer and rest my head back on my pillow. I look to the ceiling, begging for answers. *What did*

201

I miss? How did this happen? What did I do wrong?

| 11:00 AM |

<u>Thomas</u>

The ride to the funeral home is so quiet I can hear the turning of my steering wheel. Mom received a call from the funeral home this morning to come over this afternoon to discuss logistics. We had to drive two cars in order to fit everyone. I'm driving with my sisters and my mom, while Brandon drives my aunt and Grandpa and Grandma O. *I wonder if their car is as quiet as ours.* This week would be the first time Brandon meets most of the extended family and I can only imagine how uncomfortable it is to meet everyone under the current circumstances.

The GPS directs me to the parking lot on the left. As I put the car into park, I notice the busyness of the road the funeral home is on. It's between a Food Lion and a Circle K gas station. The funeral home feels out of place here; unless you had a reason to come here I'm not sure anyone would ever realize it's a funeral home.

Natalie mumbles, "This feels strange," as she closes the car door behind her.

We sit on the couch in the waiting room while Mom goes back first to talk to the funeral director. There is an oddly placed bird cage in the back corner of the waiting room. *Who has pet birds in a funeral home?* However, I can't deny, it helps distract us all for the time being. There isn't enough seating in the waiting room, so Brandon and my aunt are standing backed up to the wall. The room doesn't have much space with the couch, bookshelf, and birdcage in it. The back door creaks open, and the funeral director is standing under the doorframe. "The members of Corey's family can now join us in here."

We all stand up and head towards the door, leaving Brandon alone with the birds and a few magazines.

The director, Mark, seemed surprised by the number of people entering the room. He does a quick chair count and realizes there isn't enough seating in the room. *We all are a part of Dad's family whether it's as a spouse, a child, a sibling, a parent, or even a stepparent. All of our opinions matter and each of us feel a right in contributing our thoughts for Dad's funeral.*

Three boxes of tissues are strategically placed on the table. I can't help but be distracted by the different coffins and urns displayed throughout the entire room. *Who knew there were so many wood choices for a coffin that would be buried six feet deep?* I'm not paying much attention while my mom and grandpa relay information about the spelling of his mother's maiden name and his work title. I'm still selectively listening while arrangements are discussed and the flowers that will rest on the coffin are chosen. Suddenly, I'm focused on not completely losing it when Mark asks if we have any ideas on the type of urn we want. *No, I haven't thought about the color, shape, or design of the thing that will hold my dad's ashes. This wasn't really planned, Mark. He does realize my healthy dad just passed away yesterday, right?*

"One last question before I can show you the available rooms for the viewing and funeral. Were you thinking of having an open or closed casket?"

No one utters a word. We hadn't talked about this decision yet. *Mom must have forgotten to put it on her to-do list.*

When no one answers, Mark adds, "This decision doesn't have to be made now. You can let me know tomorrow."

My mom answers, "Okay, yeah, we haven't really discussed this yet."

Natalie offers her opinion first. "I think it needs to be a closed casket. There is no way Dad would want everyone seeing him, especially after the swelling."

She had a point; Dad never was thrilled about being in pictures and the last time we saw him, his face was unrecognizable.

My aunt steps in, "But for some people, they haven't seen Corey in years. They may want a moment to say goodbye."

Kristen chimes in, "I would like one last moment with Dad…"

Her thought doesn't sound complete; almost left open-ended.

"We could have an open casket for family, and closed to the public," Mark suggests.

I keep my mouth closed for now. The tension in the room is high enough without adding my opinion into the mix. And for what it matters, I'm not really sure how I feel about either option. However, I think this might be a better conversation to have in the privacy of our home and not in the middle of this tight room with burial items surrounding us.

The meeting wraps up, and the decision to have the viewing on Thursday and the funeral on Friday have been confirmed. In order for the arrangements to work, we will have to use their other funeral home in the next town over, about twenty minutes away. *Hopefully this one isn't positioned between a grocery store and a gas station.* My mom is recounting the items she needs to get for Mark by today in order to get the obituary posted. We kids are sent off with three catalogs from the funeral assistant. Two have urn options for us to start browsing for ideas so we can get our orders placed. The third catalog is filled with different jewelry and customizable memorial items to keep the memory of Dad alive. It's odd watching my sisters get excited about necklaces that are created based on Dad's fingerprint. *This whole shopping spree is off-putting; it doesn't matter whether the urn is $20 or $2,000, it doesn't represent Dad's worth.*

| 5:29 PM |

Natalie

The whole day has felt strange. Everyone keeps changing rooms throughout the house, not feeling comfortable in any spot. No one knows what to say to each other, but instead of allowing the rooms to be filled with silence, we continue to have awkward small talk.

My aunt will go on about how, "It looks like it's going to rain today," and Kristen will randomly acknowledge how cold the house feels as she wraps herself in a blanket. Mom hasn't come out of her room for most of the afternoon, and my grandpa is telling stories about the farms back home. When Mom's parents arrive, the increased number of guests enhances the nervousness in the house. With nothing to talk about, every attempt at a conversation feels forced and phony. I can tell everyone is trying their best to stay united and be supportive, but it's obvious everyone feels the loneliness.

I'm sitting in the living room as I listen to the current conversation around me. Thomas is talking about how old Oakley is and retelling the story of when he picked Oakley up from the breeder. I've heard this story about a million times, so I don't think it's rude if I get up and leave. *Plus, I wonder what Mom is doing.* I stand up from my chair and start making my way to her room when the doorbell rings. Since I'm the only one standing, I change directions to answer the door. *Who could this possibly be?*

I don't recognize the face when I open the door. The smiley teenager must see the confusion on my face because she immediately introduces herself.

"Hi! I'm Kate from Southern BBQ. I have a catering delivery for…"

She looks down at her notes.

"The Owen family!"

Her voice is so cheerful it makes me want to throw up.

"That's us."

My response sounds cold and unamused, but I can't help myself.

"Great! Can I help you bring it inside?"

"That'd be great."

I grab some of the bags from her delivery car and direct her into the kitchen. Everyone stands up and joins around, chiming in about how nice this is and all taking guesses on who ordered the food. *Who cares?*

205

I leave the commotion in the kitchen and head for my parents' bedroom. I slightly open the door and whisper, "Mom?"

"Hi, sweetie. Come on in."

She's in bed, but the T.V. isn't on. I look around for a book near the bed, but I can't find one. *If she isn't watching T.V. and she isn't reading, what is she doing?*

I crawl into bed next to her and tell her, "Someone had dinner delivered if you're hungry."

She greets my eyes with a smile. "How thoughtful. Did you eat?"

She seems so strong right now. I turn away because I can't look at her smile.

"I'm not hungry."

"You have to eat, honey."

"So do you," I mumble under my breath.

She grabs my hand and forces me to look at her again. "I know you're hurting, Natalie."

Aren't we all? Her sorrowful eyes are enough for me to start tearing up. I can plainly see that her pain runs deep, her mask of strength so desperately wanting to come off. I know she's worried and scared. *Not only am I heartbroken from the loss of the most important man in my life, I'm heartbroken for my Mom. The realization that I'm never going to be enough for her is crippling. I'm only her daughter and no matter what I do I'll never be able to be there for her like my dad was; she's lost her partner in life and at way too young of an age.*

Part V

TUESDAY

MARCH 26TH

- FIFTEEN -

<u>Thomas</u>

Mom called Evan last night to see if we could come clean out Dad's office sometime this week. *It would be nice to have some of the items from his office visible at his viewing.* Work was a major part of Dad's life, so it's only fitting to incorporate it into Thursday.

In the car, I can tell Mom is nervous. She keeps twiddling her thumbs to distract herself from her thoughts. My dad only worked for two companies during his entire career, and he was at the first company for about thirty years. *He gave his entire life to this company.* Even when the hours were long, it was obvious he loved his job. *I should've written down all of the advice he gave me; now I only have my memory to rely on.* He would remind us about the importance of keeping the audience engaged during presentations or team meetings. I can feel the smile creep over my face as I think about him telling Natalie and me about keeping tense situations light with a joke. *I don't think I'll be able to deliver a joke like he could or start off a meeting singing, although my lack of vocals would probably make people laugh.* He had a way of making everyone feel better even in the worst situations. *I wonder if he was the same person at work as he was at home.*

After we go through security, Mom and I are given time alone in his office. I take in the view of the golf course outside his office windows. *I remember him calling me about this view when he moved here; I can envision him standing where I am right now.* The tightness in my chest is growing stronger, so I decide to walk away before I break down.

Mom is sitting in his chair going through his drawers frantically.

"Slow down, we don't want to miss anything," I tell her.

She doesn't even look up as she answers, "I want to be out of here before anyone else arrives on the floor."

I know she doesn't want to face anyone right now, especially his direct reports. My mom threw Christmas parties and Kentucky Derby parties to get to know the people my dad worked with. She had a close relationship with his secretary and never let Dad miss an Administrative Appreciation Day. So, I open the next drawer over and start digging alongside her.

The strangest findings cause us to get choked up. His MBA degree from the University of Denver is tucked under stacks of paper. Mom recounts when Dad was working full time and working on his degree at the same time.

She keeps repeating, "He never complained. He did it for our family and never complained."

The Father's Day gift we gave him four years ago still sits in the cubby above his computer. There are pictures of all of us everywhere. Then, we find a few business cards all paper clipped together. At first I thought it was more business cards of people Dad knew, but then I notice the name written on all of them is "Corey Owen." *He must have kept all of his business cards throughout his career, reminding him of where he started.* I sit down and flip through all of the slightly bent cards. *I never told him how much of a role model he was to me.* As my regret builds, my vision begins to blur. I feel dizzy. *I need a break from going through all of this.*

As I stand up to step out, I notice my mom clutching a small book to her chest. She pulls it down to get another clear look.

"Come look at this, Thomas."

Her words so broken up, she sounds confused.

As I stand behind her, the title screams out in large, bold font.

"IT'S GONNA BE OKAY"

"It was sitting right here in the back corner of his office."

Her eyes are not leaving the title.

"I almost missed it."

Her head is shaking in disbelief for what could've been overlooked.

"I wonder who left it here."

|11:47 AM|

Dawn

I'm listening to the kids laugh at the old pictures of Corey in the other room. *It's so nice to hear them laughing again.* Going through the old photo books is too hard for me right now. I don't want to cry in front of everyone, and I know seeing a picture from when we were dating or in Tennessee for our honeymoon would push me over the edge. So, instead I listen to them go through each book while I pretend to be doing work on my laptop. Thomas can't get over Corey's old mullet and Natalie is trying to convince him to grow one out. I can't help but smile as I listen to Kristen reminisce over each photo from our Disney vacation when the kids were little.

When our wedding photo book is pulled out, I decide to step away. I head into the bedroom to look through the box from his office. *This morning was terrifying.* With every passing minute, the fear of running into someone grew inside of me. *I'm not ready to face anyone. I wonder if his co-workers will come to the services?*

I begin picking out the items to include on Thursday. Mark mentioned a table would be placed in the center of one of the rooms to display any personal items. Natalie wants to print the lyrics of the songs that remind us of Corey. Our family has been bonded by music from the beginning. When the girls were little, Corey sang to them every night. All three of the kids grew up learning song lyrics before sentences. *The memorial services honoring him have to be centered around music; it's the best way to showcase who he truly was as a person.* My fingers grip the Folsom Prison Blues album made to be a clock.

211

Corey loved this gift. I pull out every musical item Corey had and place it in the pile of items to bring to the funeral home.

I find a paper bag from our favorite food truck in Denver at the bottom of the box. *I can't believe he still has this, after all these years!* The touch of the rigid bag brings back the smell of the greasy burritos. I would skip doing my hair just to have enough time for us to get a breakfast burrito before work. My heart sinks as the memory of sitting in our car shoving our faces with burritos comes to mind. *No one would understand it, but it means so much to me.* I add it to the pile of things to bring with us.

Kristen's voice drowns out my thoughts. "We're going to Hobby Lobby to get boards!"

I wipe my face before I turn around so the tears on my checks aren't noticeable. "Okay!" My voice cracks, but I hope they don't notice.

Oakley doesn't move with everyone running around getting their shoes and wallets. I try calling him over. For once, I wouldn't mind him snuggling up next to me, but he doesn't move. He won't even turn to look at me. *I need to call the vet when the kids leave. I'll add this to my to-do list.* Another thing I have control over, one more task to do to try to keep my emotions in line.

Kristen

The mood in the house feels lighter than yesterday. Going through the photo books bring back fond memories, aiding us to laugh again. *It's refreshing to have a smile painted on my face when thinking about Dad.*

On the car ride to Hobby Lobby, we finalize each of our parts in the funeral. Natalie and I will go up together; I'll read a bible verse and Natalie will read a poem. Thomas will do the eulogy and Mom will have closing remarks. This way it will go in the order of age, plus Natalie didn't want to go up alone in case she couldn't do it. *Now I need to figure out the perfect verse to read.*

I'm searching on my phone for meaningful bible verses as we pull into the parking lot. When we enter the store, we all disperse to different parts of the store. *We want to separate to save time.* As I'm going through the available boards, I can't tell if the photos would stick to the white canvases or fall off. A store employee stops me as I'm feeling the texture of each board.

"Anything I can help you with today ma'am?"

"Oh, hi! Yes, actually. Do you think photos would stick on this type of board?"

"What type of photos? Printed?"

I adjust the board in my hands as I answer, "Yeah, just photos taken from a photo album."

"I think so! Let me show you some photo tape we have over here."

As we're walking two isles over, we begin engaging in small talk about the change in temperature outside before he carries the conversation further.

"What's the project for?"

A smile creeps over his face and I watch the excitement rise over him before he continues.

"A wedding?"

An anticipating expression awaits my response.

I stop walking as my heart falls into my stomach. *I don't know how to answer him without making the conversation awkward. I'm not even sure I can form the words.*

I manage to cough up, "Um, it's actually for a funeral."

"Oh! I'm so sorry!"

I should've lied. I look down at our feet and don't answer. *You need to stop bringing him up; you're making people uncomfortable.* The rest of the walk feels tense and neither of us utter another word. *Is this how it's going to be for the rest of my life? I won't be able to mention Dad's name for fear of making others feel awkward?*

Part VI

WEDNESDAY

MARCH 27TH

- SIXTEEN -

Thomas

Brandon pulled me aside last night asking if we could go to the mall at some point today. *I forgot when he and Natalie drove down they didn't realize they would be here for a week.* They had no idea they would have to email their professors and ask for some time off from school. They didn't pack enough clothes, and they definitely didn't have appropriate outfits for a funeral. Brandon needs a new suit and dress shoes... *by tomorrow.* So, we got up early today and headed to the mall before meeting my mom and sisters at the funeral home. Natalie wanted to stay home this morning with Mom, plus I think she wanted an excuse for some alone time.

| 11:47 AM |

Thomas

We pull into the parking lot and I watch Brandon leave as he drops me off. I notice my Mom's car as I walk towards the main entrance. *They must be inside already.*

I spot Natalie and Kristen sitting on the couch as I walk in.

"Where's Mom?" I ask.

Neither look up at me, but Kristen answers. "She's with Mark."

I make myself comfortable in the chair next to the girls. Both are looking page by page at the urn options. Natalie circles a gold heart shaped urn with

217

angel wings carved into it. *I assume this is the urn she's decided on.* Kristen falls on a simple grey, heart shaped urn that can be engraved with initials. Watching them make their selections, I notice that they don't look fully satisfied in their picks, *but I guess who can blame them?* No matter what the urn looks like, it won't be appealing to the eye. It will be a reminder of the person we have lost, the hole in our lives. *I wish there was something I could say to take away their pain.* A joke to make them laugh, or smile at best. But I know there isn't; there isn't anything I can do to help them and I think that's what hurts me the most.

Dawn

I almost run to Corey's side as I enter the room. The sight of him brings me a moment of happiness. I'm overjoyed seeing him for the first time without the tubes down his throat, without the needles pricked in every inch of his arms, without the swelling encompassing his face. I could cry from the happiness of being able to see him like this before he's gone forever. And while I know this isn't him; it's obvious his presence is no longer with his earthly body, I'm grateful for the opportunity to say goodbye to someone who looks more like my husband. Someone who can wear his wedding ring comfortably again, someone who can fit in his clothes again, someone who looks at peace.

Thomas

I'm so lost in my thoughts I don't hear my mom enter the room. She faces us all, and her eyes look like she's pleading with each one of us individually. *I can't take away her suffering either.*

"Dad is ready for anyone who wants to see him."

We've decided to see him first as a family, before making the decision on an open or closed casket. We're torn between the two options and Mom's been reluctant in making the final verdict. She wants it to be a family decision; all opinions heard and the decision to be a consensus among the four of us.

Kristen stands up, and walks towards Mom. Natalie hasn't moved an inch since Mom entered the room. As Kristen and Mom begin to walk towards the room where Dad lays, I sit down next to Natalie. She doesn't even flinch.

"You okay?" I mutter.

"I don't think I can do this."

She turns to face me as she finishes her sentence. I had no idea she was crying until I see her eyes. Her body looks fragile and weak.

"You don't have to. I can go in there and say it's a no to the open casket. They will understand."

She's shaking her head as I'm talking.

"I can't do that. I'll be the reason no one gets to say goodbye. I know I'm the only one standing in the way of having an open casket. I'm just so…"

She's sniffling with each tear as she continues to go on.

"I'm just so scared."

I pull her into my shoulder and hold her as tight as I possibly can. Feeling each tear run through her body, each deep breath she takes as her lungs search for every bit of air. All I manage to whisper back is, "Me too. *Me too.*"

When her breathing slows down, we stand up together and walk towards the room. She stays about three steps behind me as we approach the door. I reach back for her hand, but she shakes her head. "I'll be okay. Go ahead. I'll be right in."

I try looking for verification in her eyes, but I can't fully read her expressions. She looks so young right now, like a scared little girl when the lights switch off.

I trust my intuition and walk inside the room.

I don't have a chance to fully exhale before the tears well up in my eyes. *How has it come to this?* It's blatantly obvious this isn't my dad. *He looks so lifeless, but is that really a surprise?* His soul has left him. And while the man lying here looks like my dad, even with the swelling removed and the color given back to his face, *this isn't him.* I didn't realize I'd moved since I entered the room, but suddenly I'm reaching for his hand. He's cold to the touch. The temperature of his hand is clarification of his lifeless body.

I hear my sobs echo in the room around me. *I'm not making this any easier for anyone.* I turn to try to find Natalie but she isn't in the doorway anymore. *Look what you've done. You've scared her during the one moment you were supposed to be strong.*

Kristen

I walk into the room with my mom. The nerves are taking over my stomach as I turn the corner. My dad is the first thing I see when I enter the room. I'm overwhelmed by the look of him. His hands are resting too perfectly on his stomach; *it doesn't look real.* He looks like a wax statue. *How is this reality? How am I in a room staring at my unrecognizable dad?* I need his hug right now. His arms could take away any pain. *Now I have nothing.*

Natalie

I'm staring at myself in the mirror while I cry in the bathroom. Teeth clenched, I wipe away the tears. *You need to pull yourself together.* Both hands are resting on top of my head as I try to search for any strength left in me. *I need to do this.* Pinching my skin above my hand, I attempt to redirect my pain. I walk out of the bathroom before I let another tear fall from my eyes.

I peek into the room and see my mom and siblings sitting in the chairs set up on the other side of the room. No one is talking. Each of their heads hang low and they're holding hands. *It looks like they are praying, but I can't be sure.* I walk over and sit down next to Mom. I haven't been able to make eye contact with Dad. I need to make it over to my siblings and mother first. *I need to be surrounded by them so I don't have a chance to run away again.*

My mom holds my hand and whispers "I can walk over there with you." I nodded my head in agreement.

As we approach the casket, I take one last deep breath. *You can do this.* I raise my head and let my eyes focus on my dad. "He looks terrible," I screech. I slowly start taking steps backwards. Mom is surprised when she faces me.

"Really? I think he looks great."

Are we looking at the same person?!

"No, no, no. Look at his finger!"

I can't do this anymore.

"It's grey!"

He looks fake and his fingers-- they aren't even the right color!

I turn around and head back for my chair. The sight of my dad is shocking, I can't even cry. I simply bury my head into my hands and sit in disbelief. *Am I missing something? Am I being too tough?*

Kristen rubs my back and lets me sit in silence. My mom comes next to me and, without making eye contact, I know she is crying. *Look what you've done, Natalie.*

"I'm so unbelievably sorry. I thought he looked great, that's why I told everyone to come see him. I didn't want to upset you."

Her voice is frail, yet genuine.

"I didn't want to upset any of you."

Thomas responds, "You didn't, Mom. How could you have known? I think he looks great too."

Kristen adds, "I think so too."

I begin to raise my head and look at my mom. Her eyes look exhausted and her face appears to have aged ten years overnight. *I'm adding more stress to her life right now, when I should be doing the opposite.*

"No, I'm sorry." I finally blurt out.

"I was just taken aback by seeing him again."

I look to my siblings. Both their eyes are begging me to keep going on.

"He looks great, Mom. He really does."

I struggle to say each word without giving away how I really feel.

When we leave the room, my mom updates Mark on our decision to have an open casket for the public. *I know it's what my family wants. And right now, I want whatever they want.*

Thomas

Before we leave the funeral home, I tell my mom I left my phone in the room. I head back inside with my phone tucked securely in my pocket, looking for Mark. When I finally find him, I quickly tell him, "Can you please add more color to his fingers before tomorrow."

|2:34 PM|

Kristen

By now, family members and friends are slowly starting to show up at the house. When the Harrington family arrives, Mom jumps to greet them at the door. Mom and Savannah have been friends ever since we moved to Pennsylvania. Moving to North Carolina was only hard on my mom because she was leaving her best friend behind. Luckily, they have remained close and maintain their calls to catch up on each others' life.

Mom brings them into the dining room and we all gather around to catch up. I haven't seen their family in years, and it's nice to have the comfort of friends around. When Mom starts to delve into the details of the weekend, I watch Natalie tense up. She seems more than just simply uncomfortable; she looks pissed off.

I try to ignore her, but when she suddenly storms off it's hard to let it go. *What happened?*

Natalie

I run into my room and lock the door.

My knees buckle and my butt hits the ground. My head falls forward and I have déjà vu of the hospital. I let out every sob, holding nothing back. *How can they talk about this with everyone? It's enough to have the memory in my mind; I don't need to recount each aspect every time a new family member or friend comes into town.*

My heart is heavy because I know I can't tell them how I feel. I can't tell anyone how I feel without coming off completely selfish, which I know I'm being. *"Excuse me, yes, can you please not talk about the details of his death because it physically pains me every time I hear you mention the hospital or each time we recount how many units of blood he was given or listening to how he was unconscious when we had to say goodbye?"*

| 7:58 PM |

Dawn

Corey's family fills every seat in the kitchen.

I'm exhausted and ready to head to bed when the lights are turned off. I anxiously turn around, trying to figure out what the glimpse of light in the

223

distance is. Then I remember.

It's Ed's 86th birthday.

I listen to the singing slowly get louder, but I don't join in. *I can't.* I can't stop thinking about the card sitting on the nightstand next to Corey's side of the bed. I'd been nagging him for days to sign his dad's birthday card. *Now it's too late.*

I watch Ed blow out his candles. *I wonder what he's wishing for?*

Part VII

THURSDAY

MARCH 28TH

- SEVENTEEN -

Dawn

I can't sleep any longer. I slip out of the bedroom and quietly walk to the kitchen. My morning routine is important to me. This consistency reminds me that I'm still in control of my life. I start the coffee pot and water the plants inside the house.

By the time I water the last plant in the dining room, the coffee pot is full enough to pour myself a cup. I grab my mug and head to the office. The routine allows me to sit up taller in my swivel chair. I open my laptop, just like any other day, and scan through my emails. Our dentist has sent us a reminder message for Corey's upcoming appointment. *Crap. I hadn't gotten to the task of calling doctors on my to-do list.* I can feel my shoulders shrug in my self-disappointment.

The knock on the front door makes me sit up straight again. *Who could this be?*

As I open the door, I notice the Panera Bread logo on the young man's hat.

"Good Morning. I have a delivery for the Owen family?"

I'm confused, but I still manage to mumble, "Oh, okay."

I'm trying to think who sent the food when I notice the delivery man awkwardly looking around.

"Yes, sorry, come on in."

My thoughts are all over the place.

As I welcome him into the house, my eyes fall onto the mess in my dining

227

room. *I need to get this room picked up before everyone gets out of bed.* Another task I hadn't gotten to on my never-ending list. *I need to shower and get ready. I need to get my life together. What is happening to me?!*

I'm losing control.

| 3:16 PM |

Kristen

I throw my eyeliner onto the bathroom tile. *Of all days, today is not the day for my eyeliner to keep smudging.*

I can feel tears of frustration welling up. I place both hands on the bathroom counter and slowly raise my head up. I let my eyes soak in my reflection and remind myself my makeup doesn't matter. *Why am I so fixed on looking perfect? No one will remember what I look like. Everyone will be focused on something else, someone else.* My arms feel weak as I imagine Dad lying there with people circling around him. *Who will come? Will I know everyone who will be there? Am I going to feel out of place at my own dad's funeral?*

I imagine a few work colleagues will come. *It'll be nice to finally put faces to names.* I think back to the countless work stories Dad would tell us. *How will everyone react? How will we comfort people we've never met before?*

Maybe I won't have to; maybe no one from his work will come. I let my mind reflect on this thought. *If no one comes, how will we feel? How will Mom react?*

I don't know what to do anymore; my head is spinning thinking about what the next few hours will bring. I look back up at myself and before I process what I'm doing, I make the sign of the cross.

The knock on the door startles me enough to drop the makeup wipe in my hand.

"You almost done? Mom wants to head out soon."

I can hear Thomas walking away before he finishes his sentence. I'm grateful for the interruption because I have no idea who I'm praying to or what I'm asking for. I look back at the smudges on my face. *I swear if I don't get my eyeliner on this try, I'm washing my face and going without any makeup.*

Thomas

I don't look at my phone as I wait in the kitchen for everyone else. I'm not watching T.V. or even listening to music. I don't do anything I normally do to pass the time while I wait, because I don't want to speed up time. I don't want to distract myself as the minutes go by. If anything, I want to sit here in this kitchen and *wait forever.* Never go to the funeral home, never watch my sisters and Mom see Dad lying in his coffin, never greet family members in just as much disbelief as I am. *I want to sit here and avoid doing any of it.*

The noise of the door slowly opening catches my attention. I turn to face my parents' bedroom door and watch as Natalie slowly walks out. Her arms crossed across her chest, it looks like she's holding herself up. *It's apparent she feels uncomfortable and out of place in our own home, but then again, don't we all?* She slumps down in the chair next to me, and stares into the distance. Neither of us say a word. We patiently wait for the next person to enter into the kitchen, into the silence.

After nearly ten minutes of complete silence, Mom finally walks out from her room. Her eyes meet mine and a smile gradually appears across her face.

"You look nice."

The compliment feels strange considering the circumstances, but I know she's trying her best to create a more familiar scene.

"Thanks." I rub the stubble on my chin.

I decided not to shave my stubble in honor of Dad. People always tell me I look more like him when I have facial hair.

"Is Kristen almost ready?" Mom asks.

"I knocked on her door a little bit ago to tell her to hurry up."

"No big deal. We will get there when we get there."

She pulls out a chair and sits beside us in the living room. The silence returns and there is nothing to do to avoid the awkwardness creeping into the room. *Is this how family gatherings are going to be from this moment onward?*

| 4:07 PM |

Natalie

As I step out of the car, my ankle rolls and I curse myself for wearing even the smallest heel. Mark meets us at the door with a half smile. It doesn't feel right to smile back, so I redirect my eyes to the ground, carefully watching each step I take.

My feet completely stop when I enter the funeral home. The moment I walk in the door, I feel his presence all around us. *There are pieces of him everywhere.* I walk into the chapel and our photos illuminate the room. The slideshow I made is playing in every room, reminding me of better days. As the four of us slowly walk around the chapel, taking in each individual photo, no one mutters a word. *How is this happening right now?* I can hear each sniffle and the movement of hands quietly wiping away tears. *Even with the picture boards surrounding us, it still doesn't feel like our own dad's funeral.*

We make our way through the hallway into the room where Dad is lying. I can smell the flowers before I reach it; each flower competing to perfume the room. The sight of all of the arrangements makes my eyes water. *I can't believe this many people sent flowers.* We take turns reading out names as we pace around the room.

"Wow! My nursing class sent some." Kristen yells out.

Thomas joins, "Yeah, this one is from my college baseball team. I can't believe they did that..."

My mom's shocked when she adds, "Guys, this is from Dad's old boss!"

How did he find out?

I run my hands across every single card. Old neighbors, the business office of my school, my accounting professors, friends from church. I'm truly amazed at the love and support. *He is so loved; it's apparent today.*

I turn the corner, and I see him. I see him lying there, finally looking at peace for once. The flowers around him are vibrant and colorful. I take each step slowly, focusing on my breathing, trying to calm my mind before reaching him. *He looks better.* When I finally make it to his side, I reach down to hold his hand. The color of his finger releases some of the tightness in my chest. *How did they know? How did they fix it?*

|4:23 PM|

<u>**Thomas**</u>

I watch Natalie make her way to Dad, and I decide to give her time alone to talk to him. I keep walking towards the reception room to see the song lyrics and the items from his office we'd picked up earlier in the week. Before I get to the song lyrics, something catches my eyes on the table in the center of the room. I don't recognize it, and I was the one who loaded everything into the boxes to take to the funeral home yesterday. I try squinting to see if I can get a better look but I still can't make it out, so I change direction and walk over. I can feel the air inside of my lungs slowly leave as my brain figures out what it is.

I hold the Aquaman toy up to get a better look. *Who did this? Who put this here?* I turn it over, looking frantically for a note. *How did they know?*

I turn my head around, anxiously looking around, trying to search for any clues. I let my eyes focus back on the toy figure. Suddenly, I feel a rush of

231

emotions. My heart aches from an overwhelming sense of already missing him and his humor.

How will we get through life without him cracking jokes every step of the way?

|4:58 PM|

Kristen

Family arrives first. I watch as close relatives each take their own moment with Dad. Some crying so uncontrollably it's hard to console them, others still in disbelief. I watch people lean on Mom's shoulder. I listen to her comfort those reminiscing about the people they have lost. She has to be there for others even when it should be the other way around.

Even when surrounded by loved ones, I feel alone.

|5:25 PM|

Natalie

Mark enters the room to give us a five-minute warning before the public would be allowed to enter. My mom calls us over to the edge of the room.

Where do we stand? What do we say?

I feel completely out of place, and my feet already hurt.

Did anyone ask Mark how long these things typically take anyways?

Kristen

Everyone has their own story of how Dad impacted their life. I'm so overwhelmed with every detail of inside jokes or songs he would sing in the office. I'm listening intently, holding onto each word of their stories. I'm getting to know the work side of my dad through these people. I find myself laughing with strangers, crying with strangers, working through the unimaginable with strangers.

Thomas

I'm laughing loud enough to catch the attention of those further down in the line, but I don't care. Lamar's impression of Dad dancing through the security gates at work has me at a loss for words. *I can imagine Dad so clearly in his story.* I'm blown away that Dad left enough of an impression for the *security guard* to come to his viewing. I don't think Lamar knows how grateful I am for his story and the laughter he brought me tonight.

Natalie

I have to ask the woman standing in front of me to repeat her story. I couldn't have heard that right.

"I was an intern for your dad's group a few years ago, and when I found out I had to come today to tell your family the impact he had on my life."

The lump in my throat grows bigger. *He wasn't only coaching me in my life and career, he was doing it for so many others.*

Dawn

I cannot believe how many people are coming. People who worked with Corey ages ago and haven't spoken to him in years. People who didn't even know Corey but are good friends of the kids. People who have worked with Corey for such a long time, I can immediately recount several stories Corey told me about each one of them.

I turn around and grab another tissue for the person standing in front of

233

me retelling their stories of Corey. I shove down my own grief to help comfort those around me. I thought I was going to have to be strong for my kids, but it turns out I need to comfort my kids plus those coming through the line. *I need to stay strong for them, for everyone, for Corey.*

With each additional story of their personal connection to Corey, I find myself increasingly more astounded by the number of people who have come to honor him and support our family. Taking time out of their night to be with us, cry with us, and laugh with us.

|7:38 PM|

Natalie

The swollen blue eyes reflecting back at me don't look familiar. Maybe it's the dim lighting in the funeral home's bathroom, but I barely recognize the woman in the mirror. I splash cold water on my face in an attempt to make the reflection in the mirror look more familiar. But it doesn't help and in the back of my mind I knew it wouldn't. *This is how it's going to be for the rest of my life: unrecognizable.*

Before my brain can process the creak of the door opening, two women come barging into the bathroom with loud, distinct laughter. I cringe at the noise. *I can't imagine laughing again.* I make eye contact with the first blonde woman to enter. She's tall and her hair falls flawlessly down her back. I don't recognize her, but there were a countless number of people tonight, I can barely keep anyone straight. I'm exhausted and we've already run over our time by half an hour. My eyes dart between her and her brunette friend. I watch the guilt come over their faces and listen to both of them lose their breath. I cringe more as I watch them try to recall their laughter.

"We were just laughing about a story of Corey," one of the woman spits out, her voice sounds embarrassed frantically looking at her friend for back-up.

"Yeah, we, um…" her friend chimes in, trying to add noise to avoid the awkward silence which followed next.

Before either of them can say anything else, I jump in. "It's fine."

I try to show the sincerity in my eyes the best I can.

"Seriously, it's fine. He would want us laughing."

I grab a paper towel to dry my hands and cheeks as I walk out the door. *Is this how it's always going to be? Everyone feeling uncomfortable around the family who just lost their father? People making up excuses for why they are laughing in my presence? Will it ever feel comfortable to laugh again with or around me?*

Dawn

The final company are gathering their things to leave the funeral home. I look around at the mostly empty room. My body feels drained and my heart numb. A familiar dark haired, tall figured woman in the corner of the room catches my attention. *Jess.*

I race over, and tap her on her shoulder. *I've been dying to thank her since Tuesday, but it didn't feel right to do so in the middle of the crowded room.* She turns to face me and wraps me in another tightly gripped hug. *Friends are angels in disguise.*

"How are you doing?"

She slightly tilts her head and narrows her eyes as she asks. Sincerity on her face.

Not having an answer, I redirect the conversation. "I've been meaning to thank you for the book you placed on Corey's desk for me."

Her head turns back and her eyes look to the side as she tries to recall.

Her squinched eyes come back to me when she responds, "What book?"

Why does her voice sound so befuddled?

235

"You know, the journal."

Her eyes don't give anything up. *Maybe reminding her of the title will help?*

"It's gonna be okay..."

My voice trails off, leaving the sentence for her to finish.

"I have no idea what you're talking about, Dawn."

She's slowly shaking her head in confusion.

"I'm sorry, I really don't."

If it wasn't her, then who would it have been?

"Is there a way to see who was in Corey's office before I got there Tuesday morning?"

I need to know who to thank.

"No one."

Her eyes locked on mine as if the answer is obvious.

"His door was locked Sunday night. No one was in there before you."

How can this be? Surely, someone left it for me. *Corey wasn't the type of person to have a self-help journal.* My mind is racing trying to think of who it is. *Is it possible he got it during one of his department's white elephant exchanges? A joke during a trying time? Was it meant to be that I found it on Tuesday?* The irony of it all swarms around me.

Jess must recognize I need a moment alone to regroup, because she leans in for another hug. Her words softly whisper in my ear, "Stay strong. We're *always* in your corner."

I'm reminded once more, *friends are angels in disguise.*

Part VIII

FRIDAY

MARCH 29TH

- EIGHTEEN -

Dawn

The silence in the room is terrifying.

I'm lying wide-eyed in bed with complete darkness surrounding me. Yet, the loneliness of the king-sized bed isn't what terrifies me-- *it's the silence.*

This is how it's going to be when everyone leaves after the services. This is how it's going to be when it's six months later and people have forgotten to keep reaching out. This is how it's going to be when my children get busy with new jobs and new relationships.

My heart is racing with immense fear but I don't bother forming tears. I'm not sad. I'm scared. I'm scared of the unknown.

I won't have anyone to talk to in the morning when I'm getting ready, or at dinner when the kids go out for drinks.

I can barely blink; my fear is consuming me.

How many hours will I go without needing to utter a word?

| 9:28 AM |

Natalie

The clock reads nearly half past nine and I know that means we'll be leaving for the funeral home soon.

I walk into the bathroom and take one more long look at the reflection in

239

the mirror. The feeling of tears welling up in my eyes is growing as I imagine what the next few hours will look like. The thought of standing in front of other people makes my face feel warm and I know I'm blushing before my eyes confirm the rosy, red cheeks in the mirror.

I need to do a perfect job today. I can't disappoint you today… or any day of my life.

I let my mind wander to starting my job in a few months.

He was so excited for me to begin my career. He had told everyone at work about me completing the CPA exams.

A smile begins to creep across my face, before my self-doubt stops it from getting any further.

Will I even know what I'm doing or will I be a flop? Will I be able to succeed without you?

My face is getting redder. My body temperature is rising.

What is wrong with me?

I immediately redirect my eyes to the ceiling because I can't bare to see what I look like as my insecurities rise.

Is this how it's going to be for the rest of my life? I'm not sure what I'm searching for, but I keep facing upward. *Not being sure of anything without you here? Wanting to make you so proud that my expectations for myself are so high? Too high that I get embarrassed by everything too easily?*

My ears are ringing and my hands start to feel clammy.

Relax, Natalie.

I zip up my dress and hope it's tight enough to hold in all of my insecurities and doubts.

Thomas

"I'm gonna step outside for a second."

Kristen shakes her head in acknowledgement. As I'm walking outside, I can feel the vomit coming up. I race behind the trees and let it all out. *Shit. I need to get this under control before the funeral starts.* This is the third time I've puked this morning. I finish spitting out the last bit of it and wipe my mouth.

Natalie is staring at me when I turn around.

I yell out, "Jeez dude! You scared me."

She whispers back, "Not feeling good?"

She looks down at her feet and answers herself before I can, "I'm not either."

I walk over to her side and wrap my arm around her.

"We better head back in. I'm sure they're looking for us." I tell her.

When we get back inside, our immediate family is waiting in the gathering room. Mom notices our return and calls for everyone's attention.

"Thank you everyone for being with us today. Your presence gives us strength and we're grateful to have your love and support. I'd like to bow our heads and say an 'Our Father' together before processing into the chapel."

Everyone gathers into a circle and holds hands. I'm standing between Natalie and Kristen. As the prayer begins, I can feel Kristen's hand tugging with each silent sob. I open my eyes to look at her, but my mom's face catches my attention first. I watch the tears slowly roll down her face. With all eyes closed, she can finally let go of her emotions. Her disguised fear and

241

sadness have a moment to show themselves when everyone stops watching. I shut my eyes as I hear the prayer coming to an end. *I don't want her to think anyone noticed her moment of weakness.*

| 11:00 AM |

Natalie

I take each step slowly, never lifting my eyes from the floor. I have no idea how many people are seated inside the chapel, but I'm terrified to make eye contact with anyone. *I can't start crying now or I'll never be able to stand up and speak.*

Brandon

The entire room hushes as the sound of the family's footsteps come near. My heart is racing; I'm so anxious to see them, *to see Natalie.* She tries to be so strong like her mother; barely letting anyone in.

Kristen rounds the corner first. I watch her strategically take each breath. Focusing on every inhale and exhale. Her head turns towards me and my nerves intensify. *How can I help her? Should I smile? I don't want to make her cry.* As her eyes focus in on mine, I can feel my face try to offer her strength but the pain runs too deep. My mind flashes back to her on Sunday when she could barely control her heavy weeping. I try to shake the thought from my mind, and I turn away. *I can't help her; I'm making it worse. What good have I been this week?*

My gaze falls on Natalie next. Her head hangs low and she doesn't attempt to look up. I fight the urge to run to her. I want to wrap her in my arms. I want to do anything to take away her pain. My eyes begin to swell and my throat tightens as I try to hold back my tears. *I will do anything for her, I hope she knows that.*

Thomas follows Natalie in and is watching his sisters intensely. I know he feels responsible for protecting them now.

Mrs. Owen is the final person to enter the chapel. She looks so put together. She is doing a great job *trying* to be strong. However, to those who know her, her veil of strength isn't masking her grief-stricken face as well as she thinks. *I know she is suffering, her kids know she is suffering.* I think back to a quote Natalie once read me from a book she loved, "the eyes that do not weep are often the saddest eyes of them all."

Kristen

The beginning of the ceremony is a blur. I'm too busy focusing on my part and not messing anything up to pay attention to anything else. After the opening remarks and prayer, I hear the music begin to play and know it's our cue to stand up. My legs tremble with fear and the short walk to the podium is taking hours. My throat feels dry, and I'm regretting not taking Mark's offer to have a water bottle at our seat. Before speaking, I turn to Natalie hoping for a last look of reassurance to push me through. But she doesn't look up, her eyes glued to the floor. *Let's get this over with.*

My voice cracks as I speak into the microphone, "Hi. My name's Kristen."

   I guess people already know that.

I clear my throat and continue.

"And I'm the baby of the family."

I raise my eyes from the podium and I'm shocked at the number of people in attendance. I scan through the crowded rows, looking for a familiar face. My eyes land on our old neighbors from Pennsylvania. Their smiles bring me strength and I continue to move onward with my prepared speech.

"I have selected a reading from the bible that's brought me comfort during this week, and I want to read it to you all today."

A presence comes over me and I begin to read Psalms 34. With every additional word, my voice grows calmer and louder. *I know he is with me right*

243

now; he is with us all.

Natalie

Kristen sounds poised and graceful. As I stand next to her, listening to each word, I'm proud of her strength. Her voice sounds more in control with each additional word spoken of the verse she selected to read. *I hope I sound this strong.* My sight never leaves the floor, so I didn't notice when Kristen finishes and steps beside me. The silence in the room brings me to the realization that I'm now supposed to step up to the podium.

I guess it's my turn.

I see the piece of paper with my designated reading sitting on the podium just like Thomas promised it would be.

I try to clear my throat, but it turns into a cough. *Off to a great start, Natalie.*

"I have a poem by Leanne Brady I wanted to share with everyone today." I still haven't had the ability to look up, but I begin to read my piece.

"It's never the right time to say goodbye."

My nerves are overpowering my words and I have to take a break. Kristen comes over and holds my hand. Her support helps me keep going.

"We will miss you, Dad, and here is why. You taught us so much; to show no fear, to always have fun, and live our life sincerely. You were always so able, so caring, so strong. In your childrens' eyes you could do no wrong. You would always listen, and you never pried. You were the arms around us when we cried."

Each word adds additional weight to my shoulders, making me slouch even more than before.

"You never looked for praises, and you were never one to boast. You were always there for those you loved the most. We hope you can hear us so we can let you know that you were, and will forever be…"

The pause is long, but needed.

"our superhero."

Now my eyes are completely full of tears and my vision is fuzzy. I can't make out the words anymore and panic is rushing from my head to my fingers holding the paper. The poem is blurry and the paper is shaking.

I turn to Kristen and whisper "I can't read it anymore. I can't see the words."

She squeezes my hand and whispers back. "You can do this."

She's right. I can do this and I have to do this. I continue to blink hard in attempts to refocus my vision.

"So yes, today we are full of sorrow."

   That's an understatement.

"But we will smile a little more with each tomorrow."

   Will we though?

"So please, Dad, go be at rest and know--to us, you were always the best."

Thomas

I stand up from my seat and walk to the center of the chapel. *I need to be stable and steady; lighten the mood and keep the morning focused around the happiness Dad brought into our lives.* My hands are sweating from nerves and I'm terrified I'm going to puke again.

I look up and let out a loud "Uff da."

I hear people in the room let out a laugh as we all remember my Dad's famous line. The mood in the room does lighten and I know I need to continue to relieve the tension. *Dad would not want everyone crying today.*

"This is going to be pretty tough but at least it's a 'top down day,' as my dad

245

would say. As I sat with my sisters to write this we couldn't help but hear a couple of my dad's sayings, like this one: Be bright, be brief, be gone. I can't make any promises that I will be able to follow this one Dad because I don't know how to be brief when I'm talking about you."

I barely need my notes anymore. I decide right now I'm going to speak from my heart and let it all out.

"These last few days have been some of the worst moments in our life, but within that great darkness there have been some very bright moments when reflecting and telling stories about my dad."

I take a moment to take in everyone's smile. *I know each person here has his or her own story to tell about Dad.*

"My dad loved to make everyone around him smile and laugh. He would oftentimes start a meeting, or break a tense situation, with some ridiculous joke that relaxed everyone. He took great pride in his ability to deliver and tell jokes with the correct accent, song, or punch line, often reminding us kids where we screwed up in our delivery of the same joke. My dad truly did enjoy laughing and having a blast. He eventually earned himself the nickname of 'The Pusher' in most social settings because he would push people to have a great time. However, that was not the only time that he was 'The Pusher.' He pushed me and my sisters to be the absolute best we could be in our lives. I will forever be grateful that he pushed us, because he has prepared us for our futures."

I turn to them and give them a wink. *Making Natalie and Kristen smile is all I wanted to accomplish today.*

"My dad loved sports, and as much as the Vikings broke his heart, he still loved watching them. Especially on a nice Sunday afternoon with a big 'ole pile of wings in front of him, beads of sweat running down his face from the heat of the sauce, and yelling "oooh yeah!" just because the Vikings completed a 3rd down conversion."

The laughter is filling the room and I have to add, "He loved the Vikings so much that he proposed to my mom right after a game!"

I haven't seen Mom smile as hard as she is right now in so long. I smile back at her and know I'm doing my job.

"My dad lived a life that I will forever try to emulate. My dad was the perfect example for me of what a son, a husband, and a father should be."

I look down at my feet as the weight of the last line sinks in. *I'll never be as good of a husband or father as he was.*

"One final thing my dad loved was 'his spot,' everywhere he went he had 'his spot'. Whether it was sitting at the end of the Simpson's kitchen island, as we would watch Vikings football games, or the recliner in the media room, it was always the same. You would hear the heavy footsteps and then him yell out, "I call my spot"."

I take a second to find my breath before I finish.

"I find comfort in knowing that he is now entering into heaven, yelling out to his sister and his mom, saying, "I call my spot."

Walking off stage, my shoulders rest easy. *I hope I made you proud.* Mom stands to greet me, alongside my sisters. We all hug in solidarity, knowing our goal today is to make him proud and *nothing else.*

Dawn

After each of the kids' pieces, I'm amazed at how strong they have been. I finally notice they aren't little children anymore. *They don't need me to hold it all in for them.* I'm hit again with the realization that maybe I need them more than they need me.

I squeeze Thomas' hand as the four of us sit back down. I whisper to him, "I'm so proud of you," before getting up to say the final words.

My legs feel heavy and my nerves are high as I approach the podium. Everyone's eyes staring back at me, eager to hear what I have left to say.

"Thank you everyone for coming today. For supporting our family during these terrifying moments. It is so meaningful to have everyone joined in this

247

room together. We are surrounded by the people Corey loved the most."

I take a moment to smile at those seated throughout the room.

"He loved his job, and it's clear in the stories you all have shared with us."

I'm so grateful for their stories, for getting to see Corey in a new light.

"He loved his family more than anything, especially you three kids."

I'm looking directly at my kids, not breaking my gaze for a moment. *This speech is for them; to give them the strength to finish school or to wake up and go back to their job. It is to remind them to make their father proud. It serves to tell them we are in this together.*

My eyes meet Thomas. "Thomas, he encouraged your love for sports and music. He gave you your kind heart. Don't forget to keep that with you wherever you go."

He nods his head and a small tear falls from his eye.

Moving my attention to the girls, my heart aches. "Girls, you had your father wrapped around your finger from the moment you were born. All he wished for was that you both found someone who was deserving of your love."

Scanning my eyes among the three of them, I finish.

"I'm so proud of the people you three have grown to be and I know Corey is too. Be true to who you are and remember all he has taught you, and you will succeed."

Before I sit back down, I take a moment to look around at all of the people who have come this morning to celebrate Corey's life. Corey made a difference in peoples' worlds. These aren't Facebook friends; these are people he's listened to vent on a bad day, people he celebrated victories with, people he mentored. *These people love him; I hope he knew that.*

| 12:23 PM |

Natalie

Attendees exit the funeral home in a line, allowing them to give us one more hug and parting goodbye. I recognize most attendees from the night before. However, the woman next in line does not look familiar. She is shorter than many of the other women in line. Her hair is pulled back into a tight ponytail, and she hasn't looked up from the ground since she entered the line.

Must be a work colleague who couldn't make it last night.

When she finally makes her turn to stand in front of us, she reaches out her hand. The pain in her eyes is captivating and I can tell she has a special connection to my dad. Then, she introduces herself, "Hi. I'm Donna. We've haven't met in person yet, but we talked on the phone."

My heart stops. She came. *Why? How?* I have so many questions.

| 1:37 PM |

Dawn

The silence in the car is weighing us down. At a red light, I glance into the rear-view mirror and notice both girls staring out the window. I turn to face Thomas but he doesn't seem to notice. Blank expressions are plastered on all of their faces.

I have absolutely no idea what the future will hold for us. I haven't a clue how I will wake up each morning and not have Corey by my side. I can't imagine making family

249

memories without him in it. But I do know I will not let these events define us. I will not let his death destroy our family. I will not let it derail any of our children's goals, because if I do, I'll have let Corey down. We will be strong. We will keep his presence among us. We will be there for each other. We will fight through this together.

The ring is loud and familiar, yet different. I search around, trying to pinpoint the source.

Kristen speaks out, "Did anyone hear that?"

"I've been hearing that all week!" Thomas claims.

Natalie joins in, "There it is again…"

We all turn to our left, as if we finally know where it's coming from, and watch the church bells slowly sway from the Victorian church we gradually pass. This ring sounds lighter, almost peaceful. "I think our angel just received his wings," I whisper.

I swear I can hear Corey whisper in my ear, "It's a top down day, Dawn."

I hit the button to roll the top of Corey's convertible down. The sunshine brings warmth to my skin and I feel a sense of comfort. I take a deep breath and inhale the fresh air.

Corey, help me; help us. Be with us through the sunshine and each rain shower. Show us your presence on the holidays and during our birthdays. Remind us to celebrate you and hear your laughter with our own. Let us be surrounded by your love daily and use it to motivate us to live our lives for you; live our lives **with you.**

I look back at my three grown children and whisper one more thing to him, *"Thank you."*

When tomorrow starts without me,

And I'm not there to see;

If the sun should rise and find your eyes

All filled with tears for me;

I know how much you love me,

As much as I love you,

And each time that you think of me,

I know you'll miss me too;

So when tomorrow starts without me,

Don't think we're far apart,

For every time you think of me,

I'm right here in your heart.

-David Romano

EPILOGUE

-Four months later-

You're sitting at dinner with your boyfriend, watching his lips move but not hearing a word. The tightness in your throat is growing, making it harder to breathe. You try so desperately to be brought back, focusing in on his words trying to make out his voice. Instead you feel a tear slowly fall. *How can I enjoy date night knowing my mom is eating dinner alone?*

-Six months later-

You're busy at work, sitting in on a meeting when you feel the vibration from your Apple watch. It's your brother calling. Your heart aches as you ignore the call because you're too new to the job to step away. *You know you weren't the first person he wanted to call but his first choice is no longer an option.*

-Nine months later-

You're tossing and turning in bed on Sunday. Offering another prayer, you ask that your sister's first day of work goes as smooth as possible… *because you know if anything goes wrong she won't have her hero to reassure her that everything will be okay.*

-Ten months later-

Your friends keep giving you grief for not coming out anymore. Your boyfriend feels replaced by your new job. You know if you don't go home, your mom will spend another night digging through thousands of pages of medical records searching for an explanation.

-Twelve months later-

You stop working out. You stop reading. You get nervous more often, quieter in group settings. Saying you're sorry when it's not warranted. You lose confidence in your ability to make the right decision.

The weight is too much.

You lose yourself.

Overwhelmed, you come across a quote. Simple, yet powerful. Easy to comprehend, but hard to put into practice.

"You choose."

You make choices every day- what you wear, what you're eating for dinner. Some choices are easier than others, but nevertheless, *you have a choice.*

You have the choice to live your life with happiness and laughter. You have the choice to live your life in honor of theirs.

Every death is unique and profound. It's earth shattering, hard to comprehend, life changing… and I know that. *I get it.* But don't lose sight that every day when you wake up you have the ability to choose to put the best foot forward. Let every morning be a reminder that after every dark day the sun will eventually shine. Don't let your loss define your life.

The choice is yours, *it always will be.*

AUTHORS NOTES

Thanks for taking one of the most difficult journeys of my life with me.

It is important for me to note some details of locations and names have been changed to respect the privacy of those I love. It is equally important to recognize the emotions I have drawn upon for each character is fictional because it's impossible for me to know exactly how each member of my family was feeling during these devastating times. While I did communicate with family members to understand their emotions, I still believe it would be unfair to say I portrayed each thought completely and accurately.

I hope you could feel the emotions of each family member, and if you've lost a loved one I hope this book helps you realize none of the emotions you may feel are abnormal, *and you are not alone.*

This story helped me and my family process the events during the weekend of my father's death. It was therapeutic to put my thoughts in writing, and it allowed me to reflect on others' emotions during that time. I hope it encourages readers to find an outlet to help process the thoughts and feelings of death.

Writing has become my therapy. *What's yours?*

Made in the USA
Coppell, TX
07 April 2020